ears the real sense of the work. Previous attempts had strained to maintain a sense of the French style or an equivalence in rhyme and form. For all their good intentions, these ideals forced the renderings into awkward locutions or pretentiously formal tropes, making Rimbaud sound as much like a biblical elder as a modern poet. Mason has finally given us an English Rimbaud we can read as we should, as if he were kin to Jack Kerouac, to Charles Bukowski, to Jim Morrison. . . . His *Rimbaud Complete* will surely live on as the standard edition. —*Toronto Star*

"Wyatt Mason's [translations] capture the rigours of the original." —*London Review of Books*

"Exceptional new translator Wyatt Mason limns the afterlife of Arthur Rimbaud's thirty-seven chaotic years on Earth. . . . There is no small literary excitement in this, one of the best Rimbaud translations in English and certainly the most complete." —*The Buffalo News*, Editor's Choice

"A monumental achievement . . . a book to treasure." —*Scotland on Sunday*

"Thanks to Wyatt Mason's masterly translations, Rimbaud has, after a century and a half, recovered his gift."

—Askold Melnyczuk

"Modern Library's *Rimbaud Complete*, translated and edited by Wyatt Mason . . . includes all of Rimbaud's poetry as well as uncollected writings ranging from Latin school compositions to fragments of poems reconstructed by his acquaintances. This is now joined by *I Promise to Be Good: The Letters of Arthur Rimbaud*, the largest sampling of the poet's correspondence yet to appear in English."

—*The New Yorker*

"Mason's elegant translations flow smoothly off the page."

—*Library Journal*

"Wyatt Mason's translation of Rimbaud's letters is a swashbuckler of a book, nothing less than a resurrection of a remarkable life. As such, it is a worthy companion to Mason's fine translation of the poems. No admirer of Rimbaud will want to be without it."

—Arthur Goldhammer

"The letters themselves are bizarre, twisted, and oddly welcoming. . . . Mason's introduction is invaluable. It grounds the details from Rimbaud's letters in a concrete narrative, filling in gaps without the benefit of other people's return letters, the other half of Rimbaud's conversations. Mason acts as conductor, whispering into our ears through footnotes that treat their subject playfully and respectfully at the same time."

—*The San Francisco Bay Guardian*

A SEASON

IN HELL

&

ILLUMINATIONS

ARTHUR RIMBAUD

A SEASON
IN HELL
&

ILLUMINATIONS

TRANSLATED, EDITED, AND

WITH AN INTRODUCTION BY

WYATT MASON

THE MODERN LIBRARY

NEW YORK

2005 Modern Library Paperback Edition

Compilation copyright © 2005 by Random House, Inc.
Introduction copyright © 2005 by Wyatt Mason
Translation copyright © 2002 by Wyatt Mason
Maps copyright © 2003 by David Lindroth, Inc.

Published in the United States by Modern Library, an imprint of The Random
House Publishing Group, a division of Random House, Inc., New York.

MODERN LIBRARY and the TORCHBEARER Design are registered trademarks of
Random House, Inc.

The translations in this work were originally published, sometimes in a slightly
different format, in *Rimbaud Complete*, translated by Wyatt Mason, published in 2002
by Modern Library, an imprint of The Random House Publishing Group, a division
of Random House, Inc.

LIBRARY OF CONGRESS CATALOGING-IN-PUBLICATION DATA
Rimbaud, Arthur, 1854–1891.
[Saison en enfer. English & French]
A season in hell; & Illuminations/Arthur Rimbaud; translated, edited & with an
introduction by Wyatt Mason.
p. cm.
Poems in English and French; commentary in English.
Includes bibliographical references.
ISBN 978-0-679-64327-2 (trade pbk.)
I. Mason, Wyatt Alexander   II. Rimbaud, Arthur, 1854–1891. Illuminations. English
& French.   III. Title: Illuminations.   IV. Title.
PQ2387.R5S313 2005
841'.8—dc22   2005043884

www.modernlibrary.com

Frontispiece: A sketch by Rimbaud from a school notebook, done when he was ten.
The waving figure sitting in the skiff is shouting *au secours*—help!

146122990

To the memory of
Guy Mattison Davenport, Jr.
1927–2005

One must be absolutely modern.
  —Arthur Rimbaud,
    A SEASON IN HELL

CONTENTS

A DRAFT OF A SEASON IN HELL

FOUR SEASONS•95

French

INTRODUCTION

He was arrested and thrown in jail, at fifteen, for vagrancy by the Paris police. He stabbed a photographer, at sixteen, who had taken his photographic portrait only weeks before. He seduced a fellow poet, at seventeen, prying the much older man away from his pregnant wife. And yet, these famous instances from the biography of French poet Arthur Rimbaud, while true (or as true as hundred-year-old hearsay can be), only hint at the young poet's fundamental depravity, only show him splashing in its shallows. Its veritable depths, and nature, were revealed one winter in London's British Museum. On the 25th of March, 1873, Rimbaud pushed through the padded leather doors that lead into the museum's copper-domed Round Reading Room. And there, rung by a high circle of windows spilling daylight into the basin of tables—tables that would host Charles Dickens, Karl Marx, Virginia Woolf, and so many more—Rimbaud, the rebel, the blasphemer, the poet who would become famous for his "long, involved, and logical derangement of all the senses," committed his most representative crime. Its inception remains indelibly marked on the library's register for that day:

1873   March 25th

25/7   I have read the "DIRECTIONS respecting the Reading Room,"
         And I declare that I am not under twenty-one years of age.
ss. 1351 Arthur Rimbaud 34 Howland street Fitzroy square W

25/8   I have read the "DIRECTIONS respecting the Reading Room,"
         And I declare that I am not under twenty-one years of age.
sp. 1352 Henry Francis Elliot 141 Kennington Park Rd

25/9   I have read the "DIRECTIONS respecting the Reading Room,"
         And I declare that I am not under twenty-one years of age.
ss3 1353 William Frederic White
          21 Great Camden St Camden Town

On line 1351, above the day's eighth registrant (the pristinely forgotten Henry Elliot of Park Row), the day's seventh applicant, eighteen-year-old Arthur Rimbaud, in a cramped hand, affirmed that he had read the "DI-RECTIONS respecting the Reading Room"—

And I declare that I am not under twenty-one years of age.

This was an old lie from the young man, one Rimbaud had been perfecting, in various forms, for years: when he was fifteen, sending poems and pleas from his home in the sticks to famous poets in Paris, claiming that he was seventeen ("Something in me . . . wants to break free"); or, when he was seventeen and writing them again, suggesting he was eighteen ("The same idiot is sending you more of his stuff. . . . Am I progressing?"). And yet, if Rimbaud's early lies hooked him little more than minnows, the London version at last landed him a whale: a Reader's Ticket to the great library, one that settled some of England's choicest literary treasures into a boy's scheming hands. This ticket gave Rimbaud the run of a collection that no less a littérateur than Vladimir Lenin (who told his own whopper when he registered there using the alias "Jacob Richter") endorsed as having more Russian books than could be found in Russia. And with this rare abundance, not only in Russian books but in every language, what infamy did the eighteen-year-old Rimbaud then commit? What did this figure who subsequent generations of poets, the Pounds and Eliots and Cummingses (not to mention, later still, the Dylans and Morrisons and Reeds) looked to as the prototype of the bohemian poet, the rebel auteur, the sage and scourge—what, having lied his way into Alexandria, did Rimbaud then do?

In keeping with the conduct some anecdotes insist was his habit, it would not be unreasonable to wonder if Rimbaud began writing on tabletops, not with schoolboy pencils but, as some have reported he did in Paris cafés, with his own excrement. Or, in keeping with the behavior some contend was his custom, not unfathomable to suppose that he might have dropped his pants and, as some say he did into man's glass of milk, ejaculated onto the pages of the Magna Carta. Or did this famously libidinous bard seduce unsuspecting scholars? Or did the bellicose poet cleave out the pages of books with the very same sword cane's blade that perhaps pierced a photographer's belly? Or, forgoing these trifles, these low sports, having come, after all, so far—from Paris, "the big shitty," and before Paris, Charleville, the "moronic, provincial little town" from which he hailed—did Rimbaud decide, what the hell, to burn the place down to the ground?

Well, no. In fact, Rimbaud did nothing so supposedly Rimbaldean. He lied about his age, yes, but for one reason only, and not a particularly pornographic one: he lied so he could sit there, under the great dome, undisturbed, in good light, for weeks, and read.

The lives of writers are, not untypically, rather dull. A grotesque amount of time goes to waste, or seems to. Lock a man or woman in a room for ten years while he or she writes a novel or epic poem, and dinner-table talk tends to suffer, won't overflow with thrilling tales. And so, in Rimbaud's case, there is no question that his life supplies us with an uncommon quantity of entertaining hooks that might make the biographies of other writers seem, by comparison, dullsville. After all, Rimbaud did indeed write nearly all his poetry during his teens; and yes, truly, he was a serial runaway from fourteen on, hiking through France during wartime, alone; and absolutely he shoplifted; and sure he hightailed it repeatedly to Paris in the hope of being anointed by the poets he wished to have as peers; and you bet he was shot, in the wrist, by one of his lovers; and later, when he was done with poetry (for, of course, he famously said goodbye to poetry, at twenty-one, or, if not exactly goodbye, exited in the middle of the party and left the front door perplexingly wide open), he did sell grosses of guns to various African warlords. And, of course, there is his early, miserable death from cancer, or syphilis, or gangrene (for we cannot verify the cause), although we do know it followed complications that arose after the amputation of a leg, when he was just thirty-seven.

But this list of wicked plot points is, just that, a list, one I compiled in five minutes and which you read through in seconds. Rather than believing it tells us anything deeply revealing about Rimbaud's life, and instead of seeing it as proof of regular, serial upheavals, one might instead acknowledge, after scanning them, that these events, really only a handful sprinkled over a life, were, however dark, ultimately incidental, minor marks on an otherwise pale sheet, punctuation that breaks the monotonous phrase printed there that better describes Rimbaud's early life. That phrase? It says, in a repeating loop: *a man, sitting, in various chairs, reading; a man, sitting, at various desks, writing.*

And so, when we read Rimbaud's letter to a friend, in May of 1873, composed shortly after he returned from his time spent reading in London, we get a truer sense of his days than the dirty thumbnail theater his bio might suggest. Sitting in a barn in his mother's family farm in Roche—a very pastoral image that, one of well-fed livestock and clucking chickens—Rimbaud wrote to his boyhood friend Ernest Delahaye to gripe about his boredom: "What a pain in the ass, and what monstrous innocents these peasants are." Rimbaud provided his friend with a sketch, his self-portrait-as-wandering-vagrant, complete with staff in hand:

He explained, too, what he was working on ("I'm doing some little prose pieces under the general title *The Pagan Book* or *The Black Book*"). He said he'd love to send these pieces to him but cried poverty ("I already have three: *it costs too much!*"). And then, in closing, made a request: that Delahaye ship him something tantalizing, something to sustain him in the wasteland of the French countryside, for "The French countryside is death." And yet, Rimbaud asked neither for sex (in the form of illicit erotica); nor drugs (to feed his supposed program of seerdom); nor the nineteenth-century equivalent of rock and roll, whatever that might have been. On second thought, actually, Rimbaud did ask for the nineteenth-century equivalent of rock and roll, or what he might have viewed as such: Rimbaud asked his friend to send him more books.

It is a short list, but a list nonetheless and one that gives us more insight than we might imagine into those "little prose pieces" he was writing. In the May letter, he told Delahaye that "my fate rests with this book for which I still have a half-dozen horror-stories to make up. How does one make up atrocities here?" Well, it helps to have sources. Joyce could not have written *Ulysses* without Homer, nor Cummings his poetry without Sappho's, nor Pound his without both those examples and Confucius's teachings to boot—sources upon which to draw and distort, writers with whom to conspire. Thus Rimbaud told Delahaye, "I'll soon send you stamps so you can buy and send me Goethe's *Faust*... [and] see if there is any Shakespeare."

Whether or not these were sent and, if sent, received is another of history's shortfalls: we just don't know. But reading Rimbaud's prose pieces themselves, which is to say reading the book we know Rimbaud was writing that May—the book, *A Season in Hell,* that you now have in your hands—it is quite clear why he would have wanted what he demanded. That *A Season in Hell* was the book he was writing is known to us with any certainty is because, on the final page of the first edition, we find the following:

avril-août, 1873.

April-August: the season (and a half) when Rimbaud wishes us to understand that he wrote the seven thousand words that comprise the most important French poem of the nineteenth century. Not "most important" because it was the first or only such hybrid work; but because it was the first, in its content, to look both forward and backward through history and literature, using a knowledge of the two to write a poem very much about the present culture, a culture viewed, of course, through the agreeable myopia of a single reporter's gaze. The poem unfolds, therefore, in that reportorial first person, but in a language that no one would mistake for having come from the newspaper. Which is not to say that the prose is purple, only deliberate, leached of sentimentality, hard-edged, distilled into soliloquies, nine of them (the three that had been written by May; the half-dozen he wrote thereafter). Reading this progression of monologues delivered, as it were, from the lip of the stage, one could well understand how profitably their writer's time would have been spent reading, say, Lear's hoarse regrets; and Othello's proud furies; and Hamlet's half-mad calls.

Of the poem's nine parts, all but one are by the same speaker. A brief overture describes a fall from grace ("Long ago, if my memory serves, life was a feast where every heart was open, where every wine flowed") and concludes with the storyteller clearing his throat ("watch me tear a few terrible leaves from my book of the damned"). A tour of human inadequacy follows, a meditation on being that depicts, in a series of what one might more aptly term evocations than scenes, identity's destruction, the stampeding of self beneath the footfalls of history. For, at its most basic, *A Season in Hell* is very much what Ezra Pound would call, fifty years later when describing what he believed modern poetry should be: a poem that included history. As such, Rimbaud's long poem is modernism's true first throb. But the history here is personal, or is, at least, told as if history were only personal, as if civilization were always a genealogy of self ("My Gallic forebears gave me pale blue eyes, a narrow skull, and bad reflexes in a fight"). For the modern reader who knows a little too much about Rimbaud's bio, though, the poem, as it continues on, becomes harder to read. We see surprising suggestions from the eighteen-year-old, which seem prophetic: "I'm leaving Europe," the voice of the poem says, and we cannot help but think of how Rimbaud would soon leave Europe himself, for Africa and places where, as the voice of the poem continues, "unknown climates will tan my skin."

For in July of 1873, nearing that August border when we are told the poem was brought to an end, Rimbaud was shot, in the wrist, by his lover, Paul Verlaine. And yes, therefore, inevitably, once Rimbaud returned yet again to recuperate in the rural boredom of his mother's barn, sitting, we can imagine, with a crudely bandaged arm in which a hole was slowly healing, that his wounded present was very much before him as he wrote this poem. It would not be wrong, therefore, when reading the poem's fourth monologue, the only one spoken by a different voice, to suppose its tonal source, its jilted whine ("How I suffer, how I scream: I truly suffer") might have a recent basis in Verlaine, now faraway in jail.

And yet, to read the poem only this way would be a pity, for it has a larger purpose, a more mythic register and reach, one that extends well beyond the easy graspings at biography: Rimbaud was drawing on deeper reserves. A life of reading and thinking is not undone by a single shot, and a poem this rich is not explained by a single loss. Rimbaud had wanted, remember, for Delahaye to send him, in May, Goethe's *Faust*. This suggests he had the fate of the soul in his mind well before he suffered his most memorable wound. For the season Rimbaud's Hell resides in was neither late spring nor early summer; not love's loss nor a farm's torpor. His Hell was all of these, and so much more. His was informed by Persephone's—Persephone, who was stolen away to that darkness while tending flowers in a field; although she was returned safely, she could not return completely: because she had eaten six seeds from a pomegranate, that infernal fruit, she had to spend six months every year below the world. And in those six months without her, the world wilted and still does, and what is green goes gray, until she returns again from her dark season. This is a myth that rhymes with Christendom's the Fall: a taste of fruit so succulent as to leave us forever cast out from a second bite as good. Rimbaud knew these stories, of course, and now was writing his own: about the murders of experience, about the havoc of living in an unamenable world. When, ten years earlier, Baudelaire wrote his epochal essay "The Painter of Modern Life," he may as well have been describing Rimbaud's eventual accomplishment:

> And so away he goes, hurrying, searching. But searching for what? Be very sure that this man, such as I have depicted him—this solitary gifted with an active imagination, ceaselessly journeying across the great human desert—has an aim loftier than that of a mere *flâneur*, an aim more general, something other than the fugitive pleasure of circumstance. He is looking for that quality which you must allow me to call "modernity"; for I know of no better word to express the idea I have in mind. He makes it his business to extract from fashion whatever element it may contain of poetry within history, to distill the eternal from the transitory. (Jonathan Mayne, tr.)

Toward the end of *A Season in Hell,* the voice of the poem says: "I never really let myself dream of the joy of escaping modernity's tortures . . . since the advent of science and Christianity, man has been *playing with himself,* proving facts, puffing with pride every time he repeats his proofs, and acting like this is some sort of life! What subtle, idiotic torture; and the source of my spiritual wanderings." Rimbaud, like so many since, wanted to say goodbye to all that, everything that kept him from what was most human. *A Season in Hell* found a form for that forceful desire to shed what is worst in us, which is to say our puffed-up proofs. Other breaths followed, though, prose poems we have come to call *Illuminations,* fragments that were Rimbaud's last works, traces of a genius running out of time and mind for poetry. They are postcards to readers from a reader, things seen and imagined, before Rimbaud at last left the darkness of writing, finally—and we will never know whether gratefully or regretfully—behind. *A Season in Hell,* though, was this poet's great last gasp.

—Wyatt Mason
Winter 2005

CHRONOLOGY

1854   Born 20 October in Charleville, son of Frédéric Rimbaud, an infantry captain, and Vitalie Cuif, daughter of landowners.

1860   Frédéric leaves Vitalie and their four children, never to return.

1861–1869 Rimbaud enrolled in school, first Institut Rossat, then the collège de Charleville. Skips a grade, exhibiting academic gifts. Wins numerous regional and national competitions for schoolwork. Acquires reputation for excellence.

1870   Begins principal period of poetic production, which, by all signs, runs its course by 1874.

           January: Georges Izambard hired by the collège to teach rhetoric. Develops a mentorial relationship with Rimbaud. Rimbaud's first poem is published, "Les Etrennes des orphelins," in *La Revue pour tous.*

           May: Rimbaud writes letter and sends poems to Théodore de Banville, noted Parisian poet. Asks for encouragement; no response from Banville is known. In July, eruption of Franco-Prussian war.

           August–November: Rimbaud runs away to Paris, where he is jailed. Upon release, retreats to Douai, home of Izambard's aunts. Remains several weeks. Fetched by Izambard at Rimbaud's mother's insistence. Rimbaud returns reluctantly, remains briefly, flees again, mostly on foot, around the region. Returns to Charleville in November. Schools remain closed due to war.

1871   Flees to Paris in February, returning in March. War comes to a close with the declaration of the Commune in Paris, to which Rimbaud may or may not have been a witness. In May, writes the so-called "seer letters." Summer: writes "The Drunken Boat." Letters to Banville and to Paul Verlaine, another noted poet. Verlaine responds enthusiastically: "Come, dear great soul, we call to you, we wait for you." Sends money and arranges for Rimbaud to come to Paris.

September: Rimbaud leaves for Paris. Put up by Verlaine, then by Banville and by Charles Cros. Becomes acquainted with Paris literary life. Acquires reputation for brilliance and brattiness. Develops relationship with Verlaine, to the consternation of Mathilde, Verlaine's wife. Volatility.

1872   Verlaine leaves wife, flees with Rimbaud. Reconciles with wife, leaves wife again, moves to London with Rimbaud. Melodrama.

1873   Winter: Rimbaud and Verlaine in London. Summer: upheaval, ending in July in Brussels, where Verlaine shoots Rimbaud in the wrist. Police interrogate. Verlaine given a penile/rectal exam, from which it is inferred he is a participant in "unnatural practices." Sentenced to prison: two years. Rimbaud returns to family home. October: at M.-J. Poot, Brussels, Rimbaud has his *Une saison en enfer* printed; takes a handful of copies, leaving over five hundred at the shop, to which he never returns.

1874–1879 Sees Verlaine for the last time in February 1875 upon his release from prison; gives him the manuscript of the poems known today as *Illuminations.* December 1875: death of sister Vitalie, of synovitis. Travels: to London, Stuttgart, Milan, Marseille, Paris, Vienna, Holland, Bremen, Stockholm, Alexandria, Cyprus, in search of work as a tutor, teacher, soldier of fortune, and foreman.

1880   Leaves Europe, to which he will not return for eleven years. March: employed as construction foreman in Cyprus. Leaves suddenly in June, in uncertain circumstances. Later a colleague, Ottorino Rosa, will claim in a memoir that Rimbaud told him he threw a stone that inadvertently struck a worker in the head and killed him.

August: in Aden, Arabia, hired as a clerk in the trading firm of Mazeran, Viannay, and Bardey. November: sent to work for the firm in Harar, Choa, in Africa.

1881   In Harar. Expedition into the interior in search of ivory. Finds the climate in the region unpleasant.

1882   Returns to Aden in service of the firm. Ponders a change of employment. Promoted instead.

1883   Returns to Harar, now as director of the agency. Various expeditions into the interior.

1884   Firm in bankruptcy. Harar and Aden branches closed. Firm reestablished in July by Alfred Bardey. Rimbaud's services retained. Returns to Aden.

1885   Continues to work for Bardey. Sells coffee and various goods. October: ends partnership with Bardey. Allies with another trader, Pierre Labatut, to form a caravan of arms and munitions for sale to the king of Choa, Ménélik. Prepares caravan: delays.

1886   Labatut falls ill: cancer. A new partner, Soleillet, dies. September: caravan at last departs.

1887   March: finds the king in Entotto, and liquidates caravan at what Rimbaud deems disastrous disadvantage. July: back in Aden. August: Massawa, to cash the king's checks. On to Cairo for a month, where he deposits money at a branch of a French bank, Crédit Lyonnais. In Aden by the end of the year. First complaints of knee pain.

1888   Various arms caravans. Partnership with César Tian, an Aden merchant, to begin a firm in Harar.

1891   February: debilitating knee pain. March: seeks local medical attention. April: unable to walk. Borne on a litter to the coast, a twelve-day trip in terrible weather. May: Arrives Marseille, hospitalized. Mother arrives soon thereafter. May 27, right leg amputated above the knee.

            July: released from the hospital, returns to the family home in Roche. August: condition worsens, returns to Marseille. Hospitalized again, for good. Weeks pass, disease spreads, limbs fail, delusions come.

            November 9: dictates final letter, sister Isabelle at his side.

            November 10: dies, at ten in the morning.

RIMBAUD'S YOUTHFUL TERRAIN

RIMBAUD'S ADULT TERRAIN

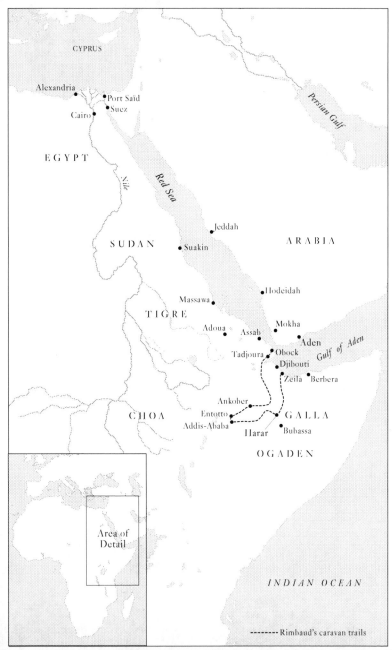

CYPRUS

Alexandria
Port Saïd
Suez
Cairo

EGYPT

Nile

Red Sea

SUDAN

Jeddah

ARABIA

Suakin

Hodeidah

Massawa

TIGRE

Adoua
Assab
Mokha

Aden

Tadjoura
Obock
Gulf of Aden

Djibouti

Zeila
Berbera

Ankober

Entotto
GALLA

Addis-Ababa

CHOA

Harar
Bubassa

OGADEN

Persian Gulf

Area of
Detail

INDIAN OCEAN

-------- Rimbaud's caravan trails

ENGLISH

A. RIMBAUD

UNE

SAISON EN ENFER

PRIX : UN FRANC

BRUXELLES

ALLIANCE TYPOGRAPHIQUE (M.-J. POOT ET COMPAGNIE)

37, rue aux Choux, 37

1873

Long ago, if my memory serves, life was a feast where every heart was open, where every wine flowed.

One night, I sat Beauty on my knee. —And I found her bitter. —And I hurt her.

I took arms against justice.

I fled, entrusting my treasure to you, o witches, o misery, o hate.

I snuffed any hint of human hope from my consciousness. I made the muffled leap of a wild beast onto any hint of joy, to strangle it.

Dying, I called out to my executioners so I could bite the butts of their rifles. I called plagues to suffocate me with sand, blood. Misfortune was my god. I wallowed in the mud. I withered in criminal air. And I even tricked madness more than once.

And spring gave me an idiot's unbearable laughter.

Just now, having nearly reached death's door, I even considered seeking the key to the old feast, through which, perhaps, I might regain my appetite.

Charity is the key. —Such an inspiration proves I must have been dreaming.

"A hyena you'll remain, etc...." cries the demon that crowns me with merry poppies. "Make for death with every appetite intact, with your egotism, and every capital sin."

Ah. It seems I have too many already: —But, dear Satan, I beg you not to look at me that way, and while you await a few belated cowardices— you who so appreciate a writer's inability to describe or inform—I'll tear a few terrible leaves from my book of the damned.

OPPOSITE: Cover of the first edition of *Une saison en enfer*.

BAD BLOOD

My Gallic forebears gave me pale blue eyes, a narrow skull, and bad reflexes in a fight. I dress as barbarically as they. But I don't butter my hair.

The Gauls were the most inept animal-skinners and grass-burners of their day.

They gave me: idolatry, a love of sacrilege, and every vice: anger, lust—glorious lust—but above all, deceit and sloth.

I find even the thought of work unbearable. Masters and workers are all peasants. There's no difference between a hand holding a pen and a hand pushing a plow. An age of hands! —I'll have no part in it. Domesticity goes too far too fast. Begging—despite its inherent decency—pains me. Criminals are as bad as eunuchs: so what if I'm in one piece.

But. Who made my tongue so truthless that it has shepherded and safeguarded my sloth this far? Lazier than a toad, I've gotten by without lifting a finger: I've lived everywhere. There is not a family in Europe I don't know. —Which is to say families like mine which owe everything to the Declaration of the Rights of Man. —I've known every young man of means.

———

If only I had one predecessor in French history!

But no, none.

It's clear to me that I belong to a lesser race. I have no notion of rebellion. The only time my race ever rose up was to pillage: like wolves on carcasses they didn't even kill.

I know French history, know the Church's eldest daughter. Had I been a boor, I would have journeyed to the holy land; in my head are roads through Swabian plains, views of Byzantium, ramparts of Jerusalem; both the cult of Mary and of pity on the cross comingle in me amidst a thousand profane visions. —I sit like a leper on broken pots and nettles, at the foot of walls eaten away by sun. —Later, I would have been a mercenary bivouacking beneath German nights.

But there's more! I dance on the sabbath, in a red clearing with old women and children.

I don't remember anything prior to this earth and this Christianity. I don't see myself anywhere but in that past. And always alone; without family, speaking what language? I never see myself in Christ's councils; nor in the councils of Lords—Christ's delegates.

What was I last century? I only see myself now. No more vagabonds or nebulous wars. The inferior race has spread, everywhere—people or, as we now say, reason: nationality and science.

Oh, science! We've remade the world. For body and soul—as viaticum—we have medicine and philosophy—home remedies and cover-versions of popular songs. Princely amusements and the games they forbade. Geography, cosmography, mechanics, chemistry ...!

Science, the new nobility. Progress. The world turns. Why wouldn't it?

Numerical visions. We close in upon the *Animus*. What I say is irrefutable, oracular. I understand, and not knowing how to explain myself but in pagan words, I'd be better off shutting my mouth.

———

Pagan blood returns! The *Animus* nears, why won't Christ help me, grace my soul with nobility and liberty. But the Gospel is gone. The Gospel! The Gospel.

I await God, hungrily. I am an eternal member of an inferior race.

There I am on the beaches of Brittany. Cities blaze in the night. My day is done: I'm leaving Europe. The marine air will burn my lungs; unknown climates will tan my skin. To swim, trample grass, hunt, and above all, smoke; drink liquors as strong as molten metal—like our cherished ancestors around their fires.

I'll return with iron limbs, dark skin, an imperious gaze: my mask will mark me as member of a powerful race. I'll have gold: be lazy and merciless. Women pamper fierce invalids returned from hot countries. I'll enter politics. Saved.

Now, though, I'm cursed: I can't stand my country. The best I can hope for is drunken sleep, by the shore.

———

But we don't leave. —We take the same roads, burdened with my vice, vice that since the age of reason has sunk its roots right into my side—climbing skyward, beating me, toppling me, dragging me along.

The final innocence and the final humility. That does it. I won't hump my disgusts and deceits across the world.

We're off! The march, the burden, the desert, the boredom, the anger.

What flag will I bear? What beast worship? What shrine besiege? What hearts break? What lies tell? —And walk through whose blood?

Better yet: steer well clear of Justice. —The hard life, simple brutishness—lift the coffin's lid with a withered fist, sit inside, suffocate. Neither old age, nor danger: fear isn't French.

I feel so forsaken I orient my instinct for perfection on any sacred image. O self-sacrifice; o magnanimous charity! All for me, of course! *De profundis Domine*—what a fool I am!

———

When I was very young, I admired hardened criminals locked behind prison doors; I visited inns and taverns they frequented; *with their eyes,* I saw the blue sky and the blossoming work of the fields; I tracked their scent through cities. They were more powerful than saints, more prudent than explorers—and they, they alone, were witnesses to glory and reason!

On the roads, through winter nights, without a home, without habits, without bread, a voice strangled my frozen heart: "Weakness or strength: Those are your options, so strength it is. You know neither where you're going, nor why you're going, entering anywhere, answering anyone. You're no more likely to be killed than a corpse." By morning, I had developed such a lost, dead expression that those I met *may not have even seen me.*

In cities, mud suddenly seemed red and black, like a mirror when a lamp is moved through an adjoining room, like treasure found in a forest. Good luck, I cried, and I saw a sky flooded with smoke and flame; and to my left, to my right, all the world's riches burned like a billion thunderbolts.

But orgies and womanly companionship were denied me. Not one friend. I saw myself in front of an angry mob, facing a firing squad, weeping incomprehensible sorrows and forgiving them, like Joan of Arc: "Priests, professors, masters: you falter bringing me to justice. I was never one of you; I was never Christian; my race *sang* upon the rack; I don't understand your laws; I have no moral compass, I'm a beast: you falter..."

Yes, my eyes are shut to your light. I'm an animal, a nigger. But I can be saved. You're all fake niggers, you brutal, greedy maniacs. Merchant? No: nigger. Magistrate? Nigger. General? Nigger. Emperor—you itchy old scab—nigger. You drank Satan's duty-free booze. —Fever and cancer thrill you. Cripples and codgers are so decent they *ask* to be boiled. —The wisest move would be to leave this continent, creeping with madness, a madness that seeks hostages for lost souls. I set out in search of the true kingdom of the children of Ham.

Do I really know nature? Do I know myself?—*No more words.* I bury the dead in my belly. Shouts, drums, dance, dance, dance, dance! I can't imagine a moment when whites will arrive and I'll tumble into the void.

Hunger, thirst, shouts, dance, dance, dance, dance!

———

Whites arrive. A cannon! I submit to baptism, dress, work.

My heart is struck by grace. And I never saw it coming!

I've done nothing wrong. My days bring no burden, I'll be spared repentance. I won't have to suffer the torments of a soul dead to decency, whose harsh light rises as if from funeral tapers. The fate of the favorite son: an early grave, blanketed with limpid tears. Of course debauchery is as stupid as vice. Cast rot aside. But no clock will ever do more than merely mark our hours of purest pain! Will I be carried off, like a child, to play in paradise, forgetting all my misfortune!

Quick: are there other lives? —It's impossible to sleep surrounded by riches. Riches are supremely public. Only divine love grants the keys to science. I see that nature is only a spectacle of goodness. Farewell chimeras, ideals, mistakes.

The angels' prudent songs rise from the ship of souls: divine love. — Two loves! I may die of earthly love, or of devotion. I've left souls behind whose suffering will swell with my departure! You pluck me from the shipwreck; are those who remain not my friends?

Save them!

Reason is born within me. The world is good. I bless life. I will love my brothers. These are no longer idle promises of youth, nor a hope of evading old age and death. God is my strength. I praise God.

———

Boredom is no longer my bride. I know these passions and disasters too well—the rages, the debauches, the madness—my burden lifts. Let us soberly consider the depth of my innocence.

I can no longer find consolation in being beaten. There is no chance of a honeymoon when Jesus Christ is your father-in-law.

I'm no prisoner of reason. I said: God. I want salvation to bring freedom: what do I do? I've lost my taste for frivolity. Nor do I need devotion or divine love. I don't repent the age of sensitive hearts. Contempt and charity have their place: I reserve mine for the top of this angelic ladder of common sense.

As for pre-existing happiness, whether domestic or not... no: I just can't. I'm too exhausted, too weak. Life blossoms with work, an old truth: my life isn't sufficiently substantial, it flies away, floats far above the bustle, over the focal point of the world.

What an old maid I'm becoming, not even courageous enough to love death!

If only God gave me heavenly, aerial calm, and the power of prayer—like ancient saints. —Saints! What strength! The anchorites were artists abandoned by the world.

Unending farce! My innocence leaves me in tears. Life is the farce we lead.

———

Enough! Here's punishment! —*March!*

Ah! How my lungs burn, how my temples stew! Night rolls in my eyes from all this sun! The heart... The limbs...

Where are we going? To war? I'm weak! The troops advance. Tools, weapons...Time...!

Shoot! Shoot me! I'm over here! Or I'll surrender...—Cowards! —I'll kill myself! I'll throw myself under a horse!

Ah...!

—I'll get used to it.

That's the French thing to do. That's the path of honor.

NIGHT IN HELL

I swallowed a gollup of poison. —May the advice I received be thrice blessed! —My gut burned. The violence of the venom wracked my limbs, left me deformed, threw me to the ground. I die of thirst, suffocate, can't even cry out. It's hell: eternal suffering! The flames rise! I burn, as you'd expect. Demon, do your worst!

I once got a glimpse of conversion to goodness and happiness, of salvation. Can I describe what I saw, here in this hymn-deaf hell? There were millions of enchanting creatures, harmonious spiritual song, peace and power, noble ambitions: what else can I say?

Noble ambitions!

Yet, I'm still here, still alive. So what if damnation is eternal! Any man who would destroy himself is damned, isn't he? I believe I'm in hell, therefore I am. Catechism in action. I'm the slave of my baptism. O parents, you guaranteed my suffering and you guaranteed your own. Poor innocent! —Hell has no purchase on pagans. —Still alive! Later, the delights of damnation deepen. Crime, quick: so I can fall into the void, as human law assures.

Shut up! Just shut up! It's all just shame and blame, look: Satan himself says that fire is vulgar, that anger is pathetic, absurd. —Enough...! Enough of errors whispered my way, of magics, fake perfumes, childish music! —And to think I already possess the truth, that I can discern justice: my judgment is sound and sure, I'm prepared for perfection... Pride. —The skin on my scalp dries to dust. Pity! I'm afraid, O Lord! I thirst; such thirst! Ah: Childhood, grass, rain, the stony lake, *moonlight when the clock strikes twelve*... the hour when the devil waits at the belfry. Mary! Holy Virgin! —The shame of my stupidity.

Up above, are there no honest souls who wish me well...? Come... There's a pillow pressed to my lips, they can't hear me, these ghosts. And no one ever thinks of anyone else. Better they steer clear. Surely I smell like I'm burning.

Hallucinations come, are without number. As before: I have no faith in history, no memory of principles. But I'll shut up about all this: poets and visionaries would be jealous. I'm a thousand times richer, and I'll be miserly as the sea. Look—life's clock just stopped. I'm no longer of this earth. —Theology is serious business: hell is absolutely *down below*—and heaven on high. —Ecstasy, nightmare, sleep in a nest of flame.

Nature's attentions only bring mischief... Satan and Ferdinand run through wild wheat... Jesus walks on crimson thorns that do not bend beneath him... Jesus once walked on troubled waters. The lamp showed him standing before us, white, with brown hair, by an emerald wave...

I will unveil every mystery: whether religious or natural, death, birth, the future, the past, cosmogony, the void. I have mastered phantasmagoria.

Listen...!

I possess every talent! —No one is here, and yet someone is: I won't squander my treasure. Shall I offer you African chants? Houri dances? Shall I disappear? Make my plunge in search of the *ring?* Shall I? I'll forge gold, and cures.

Then put your faith in me; faith relieves; directs; cures. Everyone, come—even the littlest children—let me console you, let the heart spread wide—the miraculous heart!—Poor mankind, a race of laborers! I don't ask for prayers; your faith is my reward.

—And think of me. It's worth the loss of the world. I'm lucky to see my suffering ended. Alas: my life was little more than a few mild madnesses.

Fine. Make any face you want.

Unquestionably, we are beyond the world. Not a single sound. My sense of touch is gone. My château, my Saxony, my willow grove. Evenings, mornings, nights, days... How weary I am!

There should be a hell for my anger, a hell for my pride—and a hell for every caress: a satanic symphony.

I die of weariness. Here is my tomb, I join the worms—horror of horrors! Satan, you joker: you would see me consumed by your charms. I protest! I protest! Give me the pitchfork's sting, the fire's flame.

Ah, to rise back to life! To look once again upon our deformities. And this poison, this kiss countlessly cursed! My weakness; worldly cruelty! O God have pity, hide me, I am wicked!—I am hidden and I am not.

Flames rise again, bearing the damned.

DELIRIA

I
FOOLISH VIRGIN
Hellish Husband

Hear a hellmate's confession:

"O heavenly Husband, O Lord, do not refuse this confession from the saddest of your servants. I am lost. I am drunk. I am impure. O this life!

"Forgive, heavenly Lord, forgive! Ah! Forgive. Too many tears! And, I hope, too many tears to come.

"Later, I'll meet my heavenly Husband. I was born beneath His yoke. But now, I'm someone else's whipping boy!

"Now I'm at the bottom of the world. O the women I call my friends...No, not my friends...I've never known such delirium and torture...It's ridiculous!

"How I suffer, how I scream: I truly suffer. There's nothing I wouldn't contemplate doing now, burdened as I am with the contempt of the most contemptible of hearts.

"So enough, let's confess, even if it means repeating it twenty times over—however dreary and insignificant.

"I am the slave of a hellish Husband, to him who undid foolish virgins. There's no doubt he's the same demon. He's no ghost, no phantom. But I, whose wisdom has been squandered, who is damned and dead to the world—I won't be killed! —How can I explain all of this? I barely know how to talk anymore. I'm in mourning; I weep; I'm afraid. A breath of fresh air, O Lord, if you would, if you would please!

"I am widowed...—I was widowed...but yes, I was, once, very proper, and I wasn't born simply to become bones! —He was very nearly a child...His mysterious ways seduced me. I forgot all my earthly duties in order to follow him. O this life! Real life is elsewhere. We aren't of this earth. I go where he goes, how can't I? And yet he blows up at me all the time, *me—poor soul*. That demon! —He's doubtless a demon, *for he is certainly not a man.*

"He says: 'I don't like women. Love must be reinvented, that much is clear. Women want security. And once they get it, goodness and beauty are out the window: cold disdain is the meat of marriage. Or I'll see women who seem happy, who even I could befriend, and I see them devoured by brutes as sensitive as butchers...'

"I listen to him turning infamy into glory, cruelty into charm. 'I am a member of a long-lost race: my forefathers were Scandinavian: they pierced their own sides, drank their own blood. —I'll gash myself everywhere, tattoo myself, make myself as grotesque as a Mongol: you'll see: I'll be screaming in the streets. I want to go mad with rage. Don't show me jewels; I'll cringe and writhe on the rug. I'd stain any wealth that came my way with blood. I'll never work...' Many nights, this demon would grab me, and we would wrestle and fight! —Nights, usually drunk, he'd wait in the street or a house, waiting to frighten me to death. —'You'll see: I'll get my throat cut. It'll be disgusting.' By day, he struts around like he's some sort of criminal!

"And then, occasionally, he'd speak a tender kind of talk, about remorse engendered by death; about miserable wretches who are everywhere; about backbreaking toil; about farewells that break hearts. In the dives where we'd drink, he'd cry while watching the people around us: misery's cattle. He'd prop up drunks in dark streets. He had compassion for the little children of mean mothers. —He'd conduct himself with all the kindness of a girl going to Sunday school. He'd pretend to be enlightened about everything—business, art, medicine. —I followed him, how couldn't I?

"I learned the spiritual landscape he surrounded himself with: clothes, drapes, furniture: I lent him weapons...and a second face. I saw everything that moved him, exactly as he did. Whenever he grew dissipated, I followed him nonetheless, me, executing strange tasks, far away, good or bad: I knew I would never really become a part of his world. Next to his sweetly sleeping body, I spent so many sleepless hours trying to figure out why he wanted to escape from reality. No man before him had wished for such a thing. I was aware—without being afraid of him—that he could be a menace to society. Maybe he had found a way *to change life as we know it?* No, he was only searching, or so he said. His charity is bewitching, and I am its prisoner. No other soul was strong enough—the strength of despair!—to have withstood his protection and love. And anyway, I couldn't imagine him with anyone else: we know only the Angel we're given, never another, or so I believe. I inhabited his heart as one might a palace: it was empty, precisely so no one would learn that a person as ignoble as you were there: and there it is. Alas! I needed him. But what did he want with me, drab and lifeless as I was? He didn't make me a better person, and he didn't manage to kill me! Sad, angry, I would occasionally say, 'I understand you.' He'd just shrug his shoulders.

"And so my sorrow was endlessly renewed, and seeing myself drifting further out to sea—as anyone would have noticed, had I not already been condemned to be forgotten by everyone—I grew more and more hungry for some measure of kindness from him. His kisses and his warm embraces were a heaven, a dark heaven, into which I had entered, and where I would have preferred to have remained: poor, deaf, mute, blind. I got used to it. I saw us as two good children, free to stroll through Heavenly sadness. We got along perfectly. We worked side by side, filled with emotion. But, after a penetrating caress, he said: 'How ridiculous all you've been through will seem when I'm no longer here. When you no longer have my arms beneath your neck, nor my heart to lie upon, nor my mouth upon your eyes. Because one day, I'll go far away. I must make myself useful to others, too: it's my duty. However unsavory this seems... dear heart...' Immediately, in the wake of his absence, I felt both gripped by vertigo and thrown into the most unbearable darkness: death. I made him swear he wouldn't leave me. He swore a lover's promise twenty times over. It was as meaningless as when I said, 'I understand you.'

"Oh, but I was never jealous of him! I don't think he'll ever really leave me. What would become of him? He hasn't a friend in the world: and he won't take a job. He wants to live the life of a sleepwalker. Can goodness and charity by themselves find him a place in the world? From time to time, I forget my pitiful circumstances and think: he'll make me strong, we'll explore together, we'll hunt in deserts, we'll sleep on the sidewalks of unknown cities, without worries, without sorrow. Or I'll awake and find that his magical powers will have transformed all laws and customs, leaving the world intact; I'll be left with my desires, joys, insouciance. Oh, give me this life of innocent adventure in return for the suffering I've endured. But he won't. I can't appreciate his ideals. He told me he has regrets, hopes: but they don't concern me. Does he speak of God? Perhaps I should. I'm at the very bottom of the abyss, and I've forgotten how to pray.

"Were he to explain his sorrows, would I understand them better than his derision? He attacks me, spending hours making me feel guilty for everything that has ever meant anything to me in this life, and yet, he takes umbrage when I cry.

" '—Do you see that dapper fellow, going into that lovely, little house: his name is Duval, Dufour, Armand, Maurice, something. And inside, some woman has devoted her life to loving that idiot: she's probably dead, doubtless a saint in heaven. You'll kill me as surely as he killed that woman. That's what happens to people like us, we who are kind-hearted . . .' Alas! There were days when he believed all mankind's motions were dictated by some wholesale, grotesque delirium: and he'd laugh wretchedly, at length. —Then, like some sweet sister, his maternal impulses would return. Were he less of a savage, we'd be saved! But even his sweetness is mortal. Surrendered, I follow. —I'm insane!

"Perhaps one day he'll miraculously disappear; but were he returned to heaven, I would need to know that I might glimpse my darling's assumption."

One strange couple.

DELIRIA

II
ALCHEMY OF THE WORD

My turn. A tale of one of my follies.

For some time, I'd boasted a mastery of every arena, and had found famous painters and poets ridiculous.

I preferred bad paintings: hanging above doors, on sets or carnival backdrops, billboards, cheap prints; and unfashionable literature, church Latin, barely literate erotica, novels beloved by grannies, fairy tales, children's books, old operas, silly songs, simple scansions.

I dreamed crusades, unimagined journeys of discovery, invisible republics, failed religious wars, moral revolutions, racial and continental drift: I believed in every enchantment.

I invented colors for vowels! —Black *A*, white *E*, red *I*, blue *O*, green *U*. —I regulated the shape and movement of every consonant, and, based on an inner scansion, flattered myself with the belief I had invented a poetic language that, one day or another, would be understood by everyone, and that I alone would translate.

It started out as an exercise. I wrote silences; nights; I recorded the unnameable. I found the still point of the turning Earth.

———

Far from birds, herds, and village girls,
What did I drink, on my knees, in this heath
Surrounded by delicate hazelnut trees,
And warm green afternoon mist.

What of this budding brook could I have drunk,
—Voiceless elms, flowerless grass, cloudy sky.—
Drunk from these yellow gourds, far from my beloved
Cabin? A golden liquor that makes you sweat.

I made a suspect sign for an inn.
A storm came, chased the sky. At night,
Water from forests disappeared on virgin sands,
Godly wind tossed ice upon ponds;

Crying, I saw gold—but could not drink.—

———

At four in the morning, in summer,
Love's sleep lives.
Beneath the bowers, dawn stirs
    The scent of evening celebrations.

But there, under the great oak
Near the Hesperidean sun,
Carpenters in shirtsleeves
    Are already busy

In their mossy Desert, peacefully,
They prepare precious woodwork
On which the town
    Will paint fake skies.

O Venus! For these charming workers' sakes
Subjects of some Babylonian king
Leave these Lovers be
    Leave their souls entwined.

    O Queen of Shepherds,
    Bring drink to these workmen,
    So their vigor is restored
While waiting to swim in the noontime sea.

———

Worn-out poetical fashions played a healthy part in my alchemy of the word.

I settled into run-of-the-mill hallucinations: I very clearly saw a mosque in place of a factory, a group of drummers consisting of angels, carriages on the heavenly highways, a sitting room at the bottom of a lake; monsters, mysteries; the title of a vaudeville could conjure anything.

Then, I explained my magical sophisms with hallucinations of words!

I ended up believing my spiritual disorder sacred. I was lazy, proof of my fever: I envied the happiness of animals—caterpillars, symbolic of the innocence of limbo; moles, virginity's sleep!

I grew bitter. I said farewell to the world in a ballad:

SONG FROM THE TALLEST TOWER

> May it come, may it come,
> The age when we'll be one.
>
> I've been so patient
> I nearly forgot.
> Fear and suffering
> Have taken wing.
> Unwholesome thirst
> Stains my veins.
>
> May it come, may it come,
> The age with which we'll be as one.
>
> So the meadow
> Surrendered,
> Lush and blossoming
> With incense and weeds,
> And the fierce buzzing
> Of filthy flies.

May it come, may it come,
The age with which we'll be as one.

I loved deserts, scorched orchards, sun-bleached shops, warm drinks. I dragged myself through stinking streets and, eyes closed, offered myself to the sun, god of fire.

"General, if upon your ruined ramparts a single cannon yet remains, bombard us with clods of earth. Strike shop mirrors! Sitting rooms! Feed our cities dust. Coat gargoyles in rust. Fill boudoirs with fiery, ruby ash…"

Oh! The drunken gnat in the urinal of an inn, smitten with borage, dissolved by a shaft of light!

HUNGER

If I have taste, it's for
Earth and stone,
I feast on air,
Rock, iron, coal.

Turn, my hungers. Graze
    A field of sounds.
Sample bindwood's poison;
    It merrily abounds.

Eat rocks we crack,
Old church stones,
Pebbles floods attack
Loaves in valleys sown.

————

The wolf howls beneath the leaves
While spitting out pretty plumes
From his feast of fowl:
I, like him, myself consume.

Salad and fruit
Are waiting to be picked;
But the spider in the hedge
Eats only violets.

Let me sleep! Let me boil
On Solomon's altars.
The brew bubbles up and spills
Merging with the Kidron.

O happiness, o reason: I finally chased the blue from the sky, this blue that's really black; and I lived, a golden spark, forged from *natural* light.

Full of joy, I expressed myself as ridiculously and strangely as possible.

Rediscovered!
What? —Eternity.
Sea and sun
           As one.

My eternal soul,
Heed you vow
Despite empty night
And fiery day.

Break
From earthly approval,
And common urges!
And soar, accordingly ...

—No hope.
Nul orietur.
Knowledge through patience,
Suffering is certain.

No more tomorrow,
Your silken embers,
        Your duty,
        Is ardor.

Rediscovered.
What? —Eternity.
Sea and sun
As one.

─────

I became opera: I saw that all living things were doomed, to bliss: that's not living; it's just a way to waste what we have, a drain. Morality is a weakness of mind.

It seemed to me that we were owed *other* lives. One fellow knows not what he does: he's an angel. Another family is a litter of puppies. I argued with countless men, using examples drawn from their other lives. —That's how I fell in love with a pig.

Madness—the kind you lock away—breeds sophistries, and I haven't avoided a single one. I could list them all: I've got them down.

My health suffered. Terror struck. I'd sleep for days, and, risen, such sad dreams would stay with me. I was ripe for death, and down a dangerous road my weakness drew me to the edges of the earth and on to Cimmeria, that dark country of winds.

I sought voyages, to disperse enchantments that had colonized my mind. Above a sea I came to love as if it were rinsing me of stain, I watched a consoling cross rise. Damnation, in the shape of a rainbow. Bliss was my undoing, my remorse, my worm: my life would always be too ungovernable to devote to strength and beauty.

Bliss! Her tooth, sweet as death, bit, every time a cock crowed in the darkest cities—*ad matutinum*, when *Christus venit:*

─────

ad matutinum ... Christus venit: "In the morning ... when Christ comes."

O seasons, o châteaux!
Who possesses a perfect soul?

I made a magical study
Of inescapable bliss

Think of Bliss each time you hear
The rooster's call, far or near.

Bliss has finally set me free
From desire's tyranny.

Its spell took soul and shape
Letting every goal escape.

O seasons, o châteaux!

When Bliss departs at last
Death takes us each, alas.

O seasons, o châteaux!

———

But that's over with. Now I know how to greet beauty.

THE IMPOSSIBLE

My high youth! The great roads in every weather, a supernatural sobriety, a disinterest matched only by the most accomplished beggars, and such pride at having no country, no friends—what idiocy that all was! And I'm only realizing it now!

—I was right to scorn men who never miss a kiss, parasites on the propriety and health of our women who, as a result, have been left so little in common with us.

All my disdain was on the mark: after all, I'm still leaving.

Leaving!

Let me explain.

Even yesterday, I sighed: "For God's sake! I think there are enough damned souls down here! I've had plenty: I know them all. We always recognize each other; and drive each other nuts. We see charity as a foreign concept. But we're polite about it; our interactions with the world exhibit every propriety." Is this so shocking? The world: businessmen and simpletons! —We're hardly embarrassing ourselves.

But how will the elect receive us? Many of them are insincere, given, to approach them, we muster stores of courage or humility. But they're all we have. So count your blessings!

Since I seem to have rediscovered my two cents' worth of reason—it doesn't go far! —I see that my discomfort comes from not having realized sooner that we're in the West. Western swamps! Not that I believe that all light has been spoiled, all forms exhausted, all movements misdirected ... It's nonetheless clear that my animus has every desire to adopt the latest advances in cruelty, developed since the East fell. Every desire indeed!

Well ... that about does it for my two cents! The soul knows best, wants me to head East. I'll have to shut it up if I want to end up as I'd hoped.

I cursed the hands of saints, and with them any glimmers of art, pride of inventors, enthusiasm of pillorers; I returned to the East and to its early, eternal wisdom. —However, it seems now it too has been a fetid, vulgar dream!

Nonetheless, I never really let myself dream of the joy of escaping modernity's tortures. I never had the Koran's bastard wisdom in mind. —Isn't it torture to realize that since the advent of science and Christianity, man has been *playing with himself,* proving facts, puffing with pride every time he repeats his proofs, and acting like this is some sort of life! What subtle, idiotic torture; and the source of my spiritual wanderings. Perhaps even nature grows tired of itself! M. Prudhomme was born at Christ's side.

We're brewing all this fog! We eat fever with our watery vegetables. Drunkenness! Tobacco! Ignorance! Worship! —What does it have to do with the thinking and wisdom of the East, that primitive homeland? Why bother with a modern world, if the same poisons spread?

Men of the Church say: Understood. But you mean to say Eden. There's nothing to learn in the history of the Eastern peoples. —True enough; I was dreaming of Eden! What does the purity of ancient races have to do with my dream!

Philosophers: The world is ageless. Humanity moves where it will. You're in the West, but free to live in an East of your imagining, however ancient as fits your needs—and to live well there. Be not among the defeated. Philosophers, you're from your West!

Take heed, soul. Don't fall prey to sudden salvation. Get ready! Science never moves fast enough for us!

—But it seems my soul sleeps.

Were it truly awake from this moment forward, we would be approaching a truth that, even now, may be encircling us with her weeping angels! —Had it been awake, I wouldn't have succumbed to injurious instincts, to an immemorial age ...! —If it had never been awakened, I would be drifting through purest wisdom ...!

O purity!

This instant of awakening has conjured a vision of purity! The spirit leads us to God!

Bitter misfortune!

LIGHTNING

Man's labors! Explosions that, from time to time, illuminate my abyss.

"Nothing is vanity; to knowledge, and beyond!" cries the modern Ecclesiastes, which is to say *Everyone*. And yet, the cadavers of the wicked and idle fall upon the hearts of everyone else... Oh hurry up, hurry up; below, beyond the night, will we miss the eternal rewards that await...?

—What can I do? I know work: and science is too slow. How prayer gallops, how light rumbles... I see it all. It's too clear, too hot; you'll make do without me. I have my task, and I'll be as proud as anyone else, when I set it aside.

My life has been worn away. So come! Let's pretend, let's sit idly by... O how pitiful! And we'll go on living our lives of simple amusement, dreaming of grotesque loves and fantastic worlds, complaining and arguing over the shape and appearance of the earth, acrobat, beggar, artist, bandit—priest! In my hospital bed, the stench of incense suddenly returned; guardian of sacred scents, confessor, martyr...

Then and there, I admitted my filthy upbringing. Who cares! Twenty years is plenty, if it's plenty for everyone else...

No! No! Now is too soon: to hell with death! My pride won't settle for something as insubstantial as work: my betrayal of the world is too brief a torture. At the last possible moment, I'll lash out to the right... to the left...!

And then—oh my soul—we'll have lost any hope of eternity!

MORNING

Once upon a time, wasn't my childhood pleasant, heroic, fabulous, worthy of being written on golden leaves—what luck! What crime or error left me deserving my present weakness? Those of you who believe that animals cry tears of sorrow, that the sick suffer, that the dead have nightmares, try to explain my fall, and my sleep. I can now no longer explain myself any better than a beggar mumbling his *Pater* and *Ave Maria*. *I no longer know how to speak!*

And yet, today, I believe I've finished speaking of my hell. It was truly hell; the real thing, whose doors were swung open by the son of man.

Out of the same desert, on the same night, my weary eyes forever stare at—a silver star, but without setting life's Kings in motion, the three magi—heart, soul, spirit. When, beyond mountains and rivers, will we embrace the birth of new endeavors, new wisdom, the departure of tyrants and demons, the end of superstition, and be the first to worship Christmas all across the earth!

The song of heaven, the progress of nations! Slaves, curse not this life.

FAREWELL

Autumn already! —But if we're seeking divine clarity there's no point in bemoaning an everlasting sun, far from those who die with the seasons.

Autumn. Our boat, risen through the moveless fogs, turns towards misery's port, an enormous city whose sky is stained with fire and mud. Ah... the rotting rags, rain-soaked bread, drunkenness, a thousand crucifying loves! This ghoulish queen will never relent, queen of millions of dead souls and bodies *that will be judged!* And there I see myself again, skin eaten away by mud and plague, my hair full of worms, my armpits too, and my heart full of fatter worms, just lying there beside ageless, loveless unknowns... I could have died there... Unbearable. I hate poverty.

And I fear winter, the season of comfort!

—Sometimes, I'll see endless beaches in the skies above, filled with pale rejoicing nations. A great golden vessel, high above me, flutters varicolored flags in the morning breeze. I invented every celebration, every victory, every drama. I tried to invent new flowers, new stars, new flesh, new tongues. I thought I had acquired supernatural powers. Well then! The time has come to bury my imagination and my memories! A fitting end for an artist and teller of tales!

Free from all morality, I who called himself magus and angel, surrender to the earth in search of duty, ready to embrace life's rough road. Peasant!

Am I wrong? Will charity be a sister of death?

Finally, I ask forgiveness for feeding on lies. Okay: let's go.

And not even one friendly hand! And where can help be found?

———

Yes: the dawn is harsh, to say the least.

But victory is mine: everything moderates, the grinding teeth, the hissing fires, the putrid sighs. The filthy memories are wiped away. My final regrets flee—my jealousy of beggars, brigands, friends of death, rejects of every stripe. Were I to enact vengeance against all the damned!

One must be absolutely modern.

No more hymns: remain on the road you've chosen. Brutal night! Dried blood burns on my face, and nothing is near me, only that unbearable bush … Spiritual combat is as brutal as battle between men; but the vision of justice is God's pleasure alone.

Nonetheless, the eve is here. We welcome an infusion of true strength, and affection. And at dawn, armed with fiery patience, we'll at last enter glorious cities.

Why was I asking for a friendly hand? My biggest advantage: I can laugh off truthless loves, and strike down duplicitous couples with shame—down below, I experienced a hell women know too well—and now I will manage to *possess truth in a single body and soul.*

April–August 1873

From the stack of papers Rimbaud gave to Verlaine at their last meeting in Stuttgart. The poem is "Enfance," from Illuminations, *likely among Rimbaud's final poetical works.*

Arthur Rimbaud

LES

ILLUMINATIONS

Notice par Paul Verlaine

PARIS

PUBLICATIONS DE *LA VOGUE*

1886

AFTER THE FLOOD

After the idea of the Flood had receded,

A rabbit rested within swaying clover and bellflowers, saying his prayers to a rainbow spied through a spider's web.

Oh what precious stones sunk out of sight, what flowers suddenly stared.

On the dirty main drag it was back to business; ships went to sea, piled on the water like a postcard.

Blood flowed—at Bluebeard's, in slaughterhouses, in circuses—wherever God's mark marred windows. Milk, and blood, flowed.

Beavers dammed. Steam rose from coffee cups in small cafés.

The mansion's windows were still streaming, mourning children within contemplating amazing scenes.

A door slammed, and the child whirled his arms through the town square, movements understood by weathervanes and weathercocks everywhere, beneath a tumultuous downpour.

Madame ★★★ put a piano in the Alps. Mass and First Communion were given at the hundred thousand altars of the cathedral.

Caravans left. The Hotel Splendide was built atop a chaos of ice in the polar night.

Ever since, the Moon has heard jackals whimpering in thyme-strewn deserts, and club-footed eclogues growling in orchards. At last, in a violet, blooming stand, Eucharis said: Spring Is Here.

Rise, waters. —Foam; roll over the bridge and through the woods—black veils and organ strains—lightning, thunder—rise and roam. Waters and sorrows, step forward and reveal the Floods.

For since they relented—what precious stones have sunk—what flowers have bloomed—who cares! And the Queen, the Witch who sparks her blaze in a bowl of Earth, never tells us what she knows, and what we do not.

CHILDHOOD

I

This idol, black-eyed and blonde-topped, without parents or playground, and nobler than Fables, whether Aztec or Flemish: his domain of insolent blues and greens borders beaches named by shipless waves, names ferociously Greek, Slav, Celt.

At the edge of the forest—dream flowers chime, brighten to bursting—an orange-lipped girl, cross-legged in a flood of light soaking the fields, her nakedness shaded, crossed, and clothed by rainbows, blossoms, sea.

Ladies promenading on terraces by the sea; toddlers and giants, gorgeous black women garbed in gray moss-green, jewels set just so into the rich ground of the groves, the unfrozen gardens—young mothers and elder sisters, faces flushed with pilgrimage, sultanas, princesses pacing in lordly gowns, girls from abroad, and sweetly melancholy souls.

What a bore, to say "dearest body" and "dearest heart."

II

There: the little dead girl, behind the rosebushes. —The dead young mother comes down the steps. The cousin's carriage creaks on the sand. —The little brother—(off in India!) in a field of carnations at sunset. —Old men buried upright in a rampart of wallflowers.

A swarm of golden leaves surrounds the general's house. We're in the south. You follow the red road to reach the empty inn. The château is for sale; its shutters have fallen off. —The priest must have fled with the key to the church. —All around the park, groundskeepers' cabins stand empty... The fences are so high you only see the tips of trees rustling above them. But there's nothing inside to see.

Meadows reach across to roosterless villages and blacksmithless towns.

Floodgates are wide open. O the calvaries and windmills in the wilderness, the islands and millstones.

Magic flowers buzzed. Hillsides cradled *him*. Beasts of fabulous elegance made rounds. Clouds gathered on a rising sea, filled by an eternity of hot tears.

III

A bird is in these woods, its song stops you, makes you blush.

And here's a clock that will not chime.

And here's a pit that hides a nest of white beasts.

And here's a cathedral that sinks, and a lake that rises.

And here's a little carriage abandoned in a thicket, or that rolls beribboned down the road.

And here's a troupe of little actors in costume, spied on the edge of the woods.

And when you grow hungry, and thirsty, here's someone to chase you home.

IV

I'm the saint praying on a balcony—like peaceful beasts grazing along the Sea of Palestine.

I'm the scholar in a plain reading chair. Branches and rain beat the library windows.

I'm the pedestrian on the high road through the stunted woods; the sound of floodgates drowns out my footsteps. I stare at the melancholy wash of another golden sunset.

Or I could be the child abandoned on a high seas jetty, a bumpkin along a lane that butts the sky.

The path is harsh. The hillocks are weed. The air is still. How far we are from birds and streams. The end of the world must be just ahead.

V

So rent me a tomb whose cinderblocks peek through their whitewash—deep below ground.

I rest my elbows on the table, the lamp brightly illuminates newspapers and boring books I'm dumb enough to reread.

Far, far above my subterranean sitting room, houses settle and spread, fog gathers. Mud is red or black. Monstrous city, endless night!

Nearer are the sewers. At my flanks, the width of the world. Or perhaps azure abysses, pits of fire. Perhaps moons and comets collide at these depths, seas and stories.

In these bitter hours, I imagine spheres of sapphire and steel. I have mastered silence. So what's that vent doing, up there, illuminating a corner of my ceiling?

TALE

A Prince was troubled by his habit of acting on only the most obvious impulses. He could imagine a sort of revolutionary love, and suspected his wives capable of more than mere complaisance embellished with blue skies and riches. He wanted truth, hours of complete desire and satisfaction. Whether an aberration of piety or no, he wanted it all the same. At the very least, he was willing to find out.

—All the women who had been with him were put to death. Slaughter in Beauty's garden. They blessed him beneath the blade. He sought no replacements. —Yet the women reappeared.

He killed all his followers, after hunting or drinking. —None ceased to follow him.

He took pleasure slitting the throats of rare beasts. He torched palaces. He pounced on people and tore them apart. —Yet the crowd, the golden roofs, the beautiful beasts: all remained.

Can one rejoice in destruction, be rejuvenated by cruelty? His people didn't grumble. None objected.

One night, he galloped high in his saddle. A Genie appeared, of ineffable, inexpressible beauty. His face and bearing suggested a complex, multifaceted love; unspeakable—even unbearable—happiness! The Prince and the Genie vanished into each other, completely. How could they not have died of it? They died together.

But the Prince passed away in his palace, at a routine age. The Prince was the Genie. The Genie was the Prince.

Our desires lack an inner music.

SIDESHOW

Muscle-bound goons. The kind that rape the world. Self-satisfied, in no hurry to devote their remarkable faculties to understanding another's mind. Such wise men. Stares as blank as summer nights, red and black, tricolored, golden star-stung steel: twisted features, leaden, pale, inflamed; hoarse guffaws. A grim onslaught of pretense. To hear what these kids would say about Cherubino in their rough voices and violent ways. They're heading to town to get it from behind, all decked out in sickening *luxury*.

A violent Paradise of runaway sneers! But no match for your Fakirs and hackneyed theatrics. In costumes sewn together with all the taste of a nightmare, they strut through assorted laments, tragedies filled with all every brigand and demigod missing from religion and history. Chinese, Hottentots, bohemians, fools, hyenas, Molochs, ancient lunacies, sinister demons—they slip savage slaps and tickles into your mother's old chestnuts. A little avant-guarde here, some three-hankie stuff there. Master jugglers who use riveting comedy to transform players and scenes. Eyes ignite, blood sings, bones stretch, tears and red rivulets run. Their clowning can last minutes, or months.

Only I have the key to this savage sideshow.

ANTIQUE

Graceful son of Pan! Beneath your flower- and berry-crowned brow, the precious spheres of your eyes revolve. Your wine-stained cheeks seem hollow. Your fangs gleam. Your chest is a lyre, music flows from your pale arms. Your heart beats in a belly where two sexes sleep. At night, wander, softly moving this thigh, then this other thigh, and this left leg.

BEING BEAUTEOUS

Out of the snow rises a Beautiful Being. Whisperings of death and rounds of unheard music lift this worshipped shape, make it expand and tremble like a ghost; black and scarlet wounds colonize immaculate flesh. Life's colors deepen, dance, and radiate from this Vision fresh off the blocks. Tremors rise and rumble, and the wild flavor of these effects is outdone by mortal whisperings and raucous music that the distant world hurls upon our mother of beauty: she pulls back, she rears. Oh! Our bones are draped in amorous new flesh.

★ ★ ★ ★

O the ashen face, the coarse thatch, the crystal arms! The cannon I collapse upon, through a topple of trees and soft air.

Being Beauteous: Rimbaud's title for this poem was in English, as given.

LIVES

I

O the vast avenues of the holy land, the terraces of the temple. What became of the Brahman who taught me the Proverbs? From then, from there, I still see images, even of old women. I remember hours of silver and sun along rivers, the hand of the land upon my shoulder, and our caresses in the fragrant fields. A rising flock of scarlet pigeons thunders through my thoughts. —In exile, life was a stage where literature's masterpieces were played out. I could share untold riches that remain unknown. I watch you unearth your discoveries. I know what will be! My wisdom? You disdain it like chaos. What is my nothingness, in the face of the stupor awaiting you?

II

I'm an inventor unique among my predecessors; think of me as a musician who has discovered the key of love. For now, a gentleman from a barren land and a sober sky, I try to stir myself with memories of a beggar's boyhood; my apprenticeship, days in wooden shoes, arguments, five or six unimaginable losses, and a few wild nights where my stubbornness kept me from losing it completely. I don't regret my earlier allotment of divine joy: the sobriety of this desolate landscape nourishes my wild skepticism. But because this skepticism no longer has its place, and since I'm consumed with a brand-new mess—I'm destined to become a miserable kook.

III

I met the world, in an attic I was confined to at twelve. There, I furnished illustrations to the human comedy. I learned history, in a cellar. At some nocturnal celebration in a northern city, I met women who modeled for the old masters. I was schooled in the sciences in a Paris back alley. I made my own masterpieces and retired to an appropriately magnificent Oriental retreat. I brewed my blood. My burden was lifted. My brooding was over. I am beyond all parting, and past persuading.

DEPARTURE

Seen enough. Visions confronted in every weather.
Had enough. Urban tumult, by night and day, forever.
Known enough. Life's still-points. —O tumult and Visions!
Departure for fresh affection and noise!

ROYALTY

One fine morning, in a land of very decent people, a gorgeous man and woman were shouting in the town square:

"Friends, I want her to be queen!"

"I want to be queen!" She laughed, and trembled.

He spoke to his friends of revelation, of an ordeal undergone. They swooned, one against the other.

And so they ruled all morning, as crimson curtains blazed from windows, and then all afternoon, as they strolled the palm gardens.

FOR A REASON

Striking your finger on a drum discharges all sound and begins a new harmony.

Taking a single step suggests the advent and advance of new men.

Your head turns away: new love! Your head turns back—new love!

All the children sing: "Change our fates, hobble the plague, start with time." They beg: "Elevate anywhere our fortunes and hopes."

Arrival from always, for departure to everywhere.

DRUNKEN MORNING

Goodness and Beauty, and they're *mine*! The noise is unbearable but it won't faze me! Storybook tortures! Hurray (for once) for great work and bodily miracles! Children's laughter marks both beginning and end. This poison lingers in our veins even when we withdraw to the silence of prior discord. Now that we warrant such torture, let's make good on the super-human promise our bodies and souls deserve: this promise, this madness! Elegance, science, violence! They promised to bury the tree of good and evil in the shadows, and cast off tyrannical shackles of decency, so we could cultivate true love. The beginning was begun on the border with disgust, and the end—unable to seize eternity while on the run—the end unfolds with a stampede of perfume.

Children's laughter, sobriety of slaves, austerity of virgins, fear of faces and forms from this place—be blessed by the memory of this night. In the beginning there was hooliganism, in the end angels of ice and fire.

Sacred drunken night! Sacred if only for the mask you grant us. Fair enough! We won't forget how you blessed our hours. We put faith in poison. We know how to live completely, every day.

Behold an age of *Assassins*.

LINES

When the world is no more than a lone dark wood before our four astonished eyes—a beach for two faithful children—a musical house for our bright liking—I will find you.

Even if only one old man remains, peaceful and beautiful, steeped in "unbelievable luxury"—I'll be at your feet.

Even if I create all of your memories—even if I know how to control you—I'll suffocate you.

———

When we are strong—who retreats? When happy, who feels ridiculous? When cruel, what could be done with us?

Dress up, dance, laugh. —I could never toss Love out the window.

———

My companion, my beggar, my monstrous girl! You care so little about these miserable women, their schemes—my discomfort. Seize us with your unearthly voice! Your voice: the only antidote to this vile despair.

UNTITLED FRAGMENTS

A cloudy morning in July. The taste of ash floats in the air; the smell of sweating wood in a hearth—flowers rotting in water—havoc along walkways—drizzle of canals moving across fields—and why stop there—why not add toys, and incense?

———

I ran ropes from spire to spire; garlands from window to window; gold chains from star to star; and I dance.

———

The mountain pond smokes endlessly. What witch will rise against the whitening sunset? What violet foliage will fall?

———

While public funds are spent on brotherly bacchanals, a bell of rosefire rings in the clouds.

———

A black powder rains gently on my evening, kindling an agreeable taste for India ink. —I lower the gas-jets, throw myself on the bed, and, turned towards the shadows, I see you: my daughters—my queens!

WORKERS

O the warm February morning. How the sudden South rekindled our memories of unbearable poverty, of youthful miseries.

Henrika had on a brown-and-white-checkered cotton skirt straight out of the last century, a ribboned bonnet, and a silk scarf. It looked sadder than mourning. We took a walk in the suburbs. It was overcast, and the South wind stirred rank smells of ravaged gardens and starched fields.

All this couldn't have wearied my wife as much as it did me. Along a high path, in a puddle left by the previous month's flood, she pointed to some tiny fish.

The city, its smoke and noise, pursued us down the roads. O better world, a habitation blessed only by sky and shade! The South only reminds me of miserable childhood moments, summer despairs, the awful glut of strength and knowledge that fate has always denied me. No: we won't spend summer in this cheap country where we'll be little more than orphans betrothed. I won't let these hardened arms drag *a beloved image* after them.

BRIDGES

Crystal gray skies. A strange pattern of bridges, some straight, some arched, others falling at oblique angles to the first, their shapes repeating in the illuminated curves of the canal, all of them so long and light that the banks, heavily canopied, sink and shrink. A few of these bridges are still freighted with hovels. Others sport masts, flags, fragile parapets. Minor chords crisscross as ropes rise from shore. You can make out a red coat, maybe some other outfits, and musical instruments. Are the tunes familiar, bits of chamber music, remnants of national anthems? The water is gray and blue, broad as an arm of the sea. —Falling from the top of the sky, a white beam of light obliterates this comedy.

CITY

I am a transient, and not altogether unhappy, citizen of a metropolis considered modern, given every conceivable standard of taste has been avoided, in both interior decoration and exterior architecture, and even in the plan of the city itself. You'd be hard-pressed to find the barest trace of a monument to superstition here. Morality and Language have finally been refined to their purest forms! These millions of people who have no need to know one another conduct their educations, professions, and retirements with such similarity as to suppose that the length of their lives must be several times shorter than statistics would indicate for continentals. Moreover, from my window, I see new ghosts rolling through unwaveringly thick coal-smoke—our dark woods, our summer night! —a new batch of Furies approaching a cottage that is both my country and my fullest heart, as everything resembles it here. Death without tears, a diligent servant girl, a desperate Love, and a perfect Crime, whimpering in the muddy street.

RUTS

On the right, the summer dawn stirs the leaves and mists and noises of this corner of the park, while on the left, embankments keep the wet road's thousand little ruts in violet shadow. A stream of enchantments: Wagons filled with gilded wooden animals, poles, and motley tenting, drawn at full gallop by twenty dappled circus horses, and children and men riding amazing beasts: twenty gilded conveyances, flagged and flowered like ancient coaches, like something from a fairy tale, filled with children dressed for a country fair. There are even coffins, sporting ebony plumes, beneath night-dark canopies, behind the trot of massive blue-black mares.

CITIES [I]

Such cities! Alleghenies and Lebanons out of a dream, staged and scaled for a people their equal. Chalets of crystal and wood move on invisible pulleys and rails. Bordered by colossi and copper palms, ancient craters bellow melodiously through flames. Feasts of love ring out across canals strung behind the chalets. A pack of pealing bells calls from the gorges. Guilds of gigantic singers gather, wearing clothes and bearing banners as dazzling as light from the summits. On platforms in passes, Rolands sound their valor. On footbridges spanning abysses and rooftops of inns, the ardent sky ignites flagpoles. The collapse of old apotheoses joins heaven to earth, fields where seraphic centauresses gambol and dance between avalanches. A sea freighted with orphic fleets and rumbling pearls and precious conches unfolds above the highest peaks, disturbed by Venus' perpetual birth—a sea that sometimes darkens with fatal flashes. Harvested flowers as big as guns and goblets are lowing on the hillsides. Parades of Mabs climb the ravine in red and opaline dresses. Up above, their feet in the falls and brambles, stags suckle Diana's breasts. Suburban Bacchantes sob, the moon burns and bawls. Venus visits the caves of blacksmiths and hermits. Groups of belfries sing the people's ideas. Unfamiliar music escapes from castles of bone. All the old mythologies gambol and dance, and urges, like elk, stampede through the streets. The Paradise of storms collapses. Savages dance ceaselessly at the feast of night. And, once, I even descended into the flow of a Baghdad boulevard where groups were singing joyously of new work, blown by a thick breeze, moving around but unable to elude the fabulous ghosts of the mountains where we must have met.

What fine arms and hour will return this region to me, whence my slumbers and slightest movements come?

VAGABONDS

Pathetic brother! What wretched sleepless nights he caused! "I had little passion for this undertaking. I played to his weaknesses. If we returned to exile, to slavery, I would be to blame." He believed, strangely, I was both jinxed and innocent. His reasons were disturbing.

I responded by snickering at this satanic doctor, and fleeing out the window. Beyond a countryside singing with strains of singular music, I created ghosts of future, nocturnal luxury.

After this vaguely hygienic distraction, I would relax on my pallet. And, nearly every night, just as I had fallen asleep, this poor brother would rise, mouth dry, eyes bulging—just as he'd dreamed—and drag me into the next room while screaming his idiotic sorrowful dream.

Essentially, sincerely, I had taken it upon myself to return him to his primitive, sun-worshipping state—and we wandered, sustained by wine from cellars and the road's dry bread—as I impatiently sought means and ends.

CITIES [II]

The official acropolis surpasses our most colossal conceptions of modern barbarity. Impossible to adequately describe the flat daylight produced by this immutably gray sky, the imperial sheen of the edifices, and the eternal snow on the ground. With a singular taste for enormity, they reproduced all the marvels of classical architecture. I attend painting expositions in places twenty times larger than Hampton Court. And what paintings! A Norwegian Nebuchadnezzar built the staircases of the government buildings; the underlings I was able to see are already haughtier than Brahmins, and I trembled as guards and construction foremen passed outside the colossi. As the buildings were sited along squares, closed courtyards and terraces within, traffic has been shut out. The parks are displays of nature at its most primitive, artfully laid out. Some of the upper parts of town are inexplicable: a boatless arm of the sea unrolls its blue sleeve of delicate hail between piers loaded with giant candelabras. A short bridge leads to a postern directly beneath the dome of Sainte-Chapelle. This dome is an artistic steel frame roughly fifteen thousand feet wide.

From certain points on the copper footbridges, platforms, and staircases that wind through the markets and around pillars, I thought I could judge the depth of the city! One marvel I couldn't reconcile: are the city's other regions above or beneath the level of the acropolis? Reconnaissance is impossible for the tourist of today. The commercial quarter is a circus in a single style: arcaded galleries. You can't see shops, but the snow on sidewalks is trampled; a few nabobs—as rare as pedestrians on a London Sunday morning—make their way towards a diamond diligence. A few red velvet divans: ice cold drinks are served, running eight hundred to eight thousand rupees. I start to look for a theater in this circus, but I realize that the shops fill with dark dramas all their own. There must be a police presence. But the law must be sufficiently strange here that I abandon imagining what local adventurers are like.

The suburb, as elegant as a beautiful Paris street, enjoys luminous light. The local democrats number a few hundred souls. Here, again, the houses aren't in rows; the suburb loses itself strangely in the countryside, the "Country" that fills the eternal West with forests and endless plantations where savage gentlemen seek distraction beneath the light they made.

VIGILS

I

Enlightened leisure, neither fever nor languor, in a meadow or a bed.
A friend neither ardent nor weak. A friend.
A love neither tormenting nor tormented. A love.
The air and the world, unsought. A life.
—Was this it?
—And the dream grows cool.

II

Lightning returns to the branches of the building. From opposite ends of the room, whatever the setting, harmonic elevations merge. The wall before the watcher is a psychological succession of parts of friezes, atmospheric sections, and geological strata. —A dream, intense and swift, of sentimental groups, people of every possible character amidst every possible appearance.

III

At night, the lamps and rugs of the vigil make the sounds of waves along keel and steerage.

The sea of the vigil, like Amélie's breasts.

The tapestries hang halfway up, the doves of the vigil plunge into a thicket of emerald lace.

.   .   .   .

The back of black hearth, real suns from shorelines: Ah! magical wells; only a glimpse of dawn, this time.

MYSTIC

On the hillside, angels twirl their wool dresses through pastures of emerald and steel.

Meadows of flame leap to the hillock's crest. On the left, its humus has been trampled by murders and battles, disastrous noises etch a map of the terrain. Behind the crest to the right is a line leading to the Orient, to progress.

And while the band running across the top of the image is made by the spinning and leaping sound heard in conches and human nights . . .

The blossoming sweetness of stars and sky and all the rest falls in front of the hillside before us like a basket—and turns the abyss below to blossom and blue.

DAWN

I held the summer dawn in my arms.

Nothing stirred in front of the palaces. The water was dead. Camps of shadows rested on the road through the woods. I walked, awakening live warm breaths as precious stones looked on and wings soundlessly rose.

The first undertaking, in a path already filled with cool pale glimmers of light, was a flower that told me its name.

I laughed at a blonde *wasserfall* whose tresses streamed between firs; at the silvered summit I recognized the goddess.

So, one by one, I lifted her veils. In a lane, whirling my arms. In a field, shouting to a rooster. Into the city she fled, between steeples and domes, and I gave chase, running like a beggar on marble docks.

At the crest of the road, near a stand of laurels, I enveloped her in her gathered veils, and felt something of her boundless shape. Dawn and the child fell to the forest floor.

It was noon when I awoke.

FLOWERS

From a golden slope—among silk ropes, gray veils, green velvets, and crystal discs that blacken like the bronze of the sun—I watch the foxglove open on a carpet of silver filigree, eyes and hair.

Pieces of yellow gold scattered over agate, mahogany pillars supporting an emerald dome, bouquets of white satin and delicate sprays of rubies surround the water-rose.

Like some god's enormous blue eyes staring from within a silhouette of snow, sea and sky attract a crowd of strong young roses to the marble steps.

COMMON NOCTURNE

A breath of air opens operatic breaches in walls—rotten rooftops reel—hearths are sundered—casements covered. —One foot braced on a gargoyle, I cut through the vineyard in a carriage whose age is fixed by its convex mirrors, its curved woodwork, and contoured seats. A cloistered hearse of sleep, a cabin for my nonsense, the carriage veers onto the grass, away from the highway: and through an imperfection, high in the window on the right, spin pale lunar forms, leaves, breasts; —A deep green and blue invade the scene.

Unharnessing by a gravel patch.

—Here we'll whistle for the storm, for Sodoms—for Solymas—for wild beasts and armies,

(—Will coachmen and animals from some dream exit the airless woods to thrust me, up to my eyes, beneath the surface of a silken source?)

—And send us off, whipped by lapping waters and spilled drinks, to the howls of mastiffs...

—A breath of air, and hearths are sundered.

SEASCAPE

Chariots of silver and copper—
Prows of silver and steel—
Beat foam—
Stirring stumps of bramble—
Currents from the moor,
And the vast ruts of the tidal ebb
Flow eastward, circularly,
Towards the pillars of the forest—
Towards the pilings of the pier,
Whose corner is struck
By whirlwinds of light.

WINTER CELEBRATED

The waterfall sings behind opera-buffa shacks. Girandoles prolong sunset's greens and reds across orchards and paths by the river Meander. Nymphs out of Horace with First Empire coifs—Siberian dances, Chinese ladies out of Boucher.

ANGUISH

Might it be She could forgive my eternally dashed ambitions; in the end, can wealth make up for ages of indigence; can a day of success absolve the shame of my fatal incompetence?

(O palms and diamonds! —Love and strength! Greatest joys and glories! Of every type and place—demon, god—this being's youth: myself!)

Can accidents of scientific fantasy and organizations of social brotherhood be cherished as the progressive restitution of our earliest liberty?

But the Vampire who keeps us in line decrees we must amuse ourselves with what she leaves—that or start telling jokes.

So let me wallow in my wounds, in heavy air and sea; tormented by watery silence and murderous air; tortures that jeer at me, atrociously, in stormy silence.

METROPOLITAN

From indigo straights to Ossian seas, on pink and orange sands bathed by a wine-dark sky, crystal boulevards have sprung up and intersected, settled soon after by poor young families who buy food from street vendors. Nothing fancy.

—Cities!

Helmets, wheels, barges, buttocks—all flee the asphalt desert in a ragtag line, sheets of fog paper the sky with unbearable layers, curving, withdrawing, falling, made of the most sinister black smoke the mourning sea could muster.

—Battles!

Look up: the arched wooden bridge; Samaria's last vegetable gardens; masks lit by the lantern whipped by the cold night; a stupid water nymph in an ugly dress, at the bottom of the river; luminous skulls in the rows of peas—other phantasmagoria.

—Country.

Roads lined with fences, and walls barely containing their copses, brutal flowers called *hearts and sisters*, Damascus languidly damned, property belonging to fairy-tale aristocracies straight out of the Rhineland, Japan, Guarani, still attuned to ancient musics—inns never to open again—and princesses, and if you aren't too overcome, stars for you to study.

—Sky.

The morning when you struggled through the snow-glare with Her: green lips, ice, black flags, blue beams of light, purple perfumes of polar sun.

—Your strength.

BARBARIAN

Long after the seasons and days, the living and land,

A flag of flesh, bleeding over silken seas and arctic flowers (they do not exist).

Surviving old heroic fanfares still assaulting hearts and heads, far from earlier assassins.

A flag of flesh, bleeding over silken seas and arctic flowers (they do not exist).

Such sweetness!

Infernos hailing frosty gusts—such sweetness! Fires in a rain of diamond wind, tossed by an earthly heart, endlessly burned to black, for us.

—O world!

(Far from the old retreats and fires we hear and smell.)

Infernos and seafoam. Music, drifting abysses, icicles clashing with stars.

O Sweetness; O world; O music! And look: shapes; hair and eyes, floating. And white tears, boiling. O sweetness! And a feminine voice at volcanic depths, in arctic caves.

A flag...

FAIRY

In starry silence, virgin shadow, and impassive light, ornamental saps conspired for Hélène. Summer's ardor was entrusted to songless birds, and the predictable languor to a priceless funeral barge adrift in coves of dead loves and sunken scents.

—After the time when lumberwomen sang to the torrent's rumblings under the forest's ruins, after beastly bells rang, in valleys, and after cries from the steppes.

Fur and shadow shook, for Hélène's childhood—along with the breasts of the poor and the legends of the sky.

And her eyes and her dancing were better still than bursts of precious light, convincing cold, and even the pleasure of the singular setting and time.

Fairy: Rimbaud's title for this poem was in English, as given.

WAR

As a child, certain skies sharpened my sight: their varied temperaments refined my face. Phenomena awoke. —Now, the endless rise of moments and mathematical infinities chase me through a world where I suffer every civil success, respected by strange children and subjected to limitless affection. —I dream of war, of might and right, of utterly unforeseeable logic.

It's as simple as a musical phrase.

ADVT.

For sale: what the Jews haven't sold, what neither nobles nor criminals have dared, what remains unknown to both wicked love and society's infernal probity: what neither time nor science need notice:

Reconditioned Voices; the brotherly awakening of all choral and orchestral energies and their instantaneous outcry; rare opportunity to liberate our senses!

For sale: priceless Bodies—ignore race, world, sex, lineage! Riches rising to meet every step! A flood of diamonds, undammed.

For sale: anarchy for everyone, satisfaction guaranteed to those with irreproachable taste; gruesome death guaranteed for lovers and zealots!

For sale: living places and leaving places, sports, extravaganzas and creature comforts, and all the noise, movement, and hope they foment!

For sale: mathematical certainties and astonishing harmonic leaps. Unimaginable discoveries and terminologies—available now.

Wild, tireless bounds towards invisible splendor, intangible delight—alarming secrets for every vice—and the frightening gaiety of crowds.

For sale: Bodies; voices; incalculable, inarguable riches—that will never be sold. Vendors keep selling! Salesmen have nothing but time.

YOUTH

I
Sunday

Beneath the sky's unalterable collapse, memories and rhythms fill house, head, and spirit, as soon as all the number crunching is set aside.

— A horse bolts across the suburban earth, through gardens and lumberyards, stabbed by carbonic plague. Somewhere in the world, a histrionic woman sighs after unforeseen abandonment. Desperadoes pine for storm, injury, and debauch. Along rivers, little children choke down curses.

Let us return to our studies, despite the clamor of all-consuming work that collects and mounts in the masses.

II
Sonnet

Man of ordinary make, flesh
was it not once a fruit hanging in the orchard—o
days of youth! the body a treasure to squander—o
to love, a peril or power of the Psyche? Earth
had slopes fertile with princes and artists,
and your descendants and race drove you
to crimes and to mourning: the world, your fortune
and your peril. But now, this work done, you, your calculations,
—you, your impatience—are but dance and
voice, neither fixed nor forced, whether season
for a double event: invention and success
—a humanity both brotherly and singular, throughout a universe

without a face—might and right reflecting both dance
and voice, a voice we're only beginning to hear.

III
At Twenty

Instructive voices exiled . . . Naïve body bitterly sober . . . —Adagio.

Ah the infinite egotism of adolescence! The studious optimism: that summer, the world was filled with flowers! Dying airs and dying shapes . . . A choir to soothe impotence and absence! A choir of glasses, of nocturnal melodies . . . Now nerves begin the hunt.

IV

Enough of this temptation of St. Anthony. The struggle against failing zeal, tics of puerile pride, terror, and collapse.

But you'll return to the task: every harmonic and architectural possibility will stir within you. Unbidden, perfect creatures will present themselves for your use. As if a dream, the curiosity of old crowds and idle luxuries will collect around you. Your memory and your senses will be nourishment for your creativity. What will become of the world when you leave? No matter what happens, no trace of now will remain.

PROMONTORY

Golden dawn and shivering night find our brig along the coast of this villa and its grounds that form a promontory as vast as Epirus and the Peloponnesus or the great islands of Japan or Arabia! Temples illuminated by the return of processions; sweeping views of coastal fortifications; dunes inscribed with the hot flowers of bacchanal; Carthaginian canals and embankments of a degenerate Venice; faint eruptions of Etnas, crevasses of flowers and glacial waters, washhouses settled in stands of German poplars; strange parks, hillsides hung with heads of Japanese trees, and circular facades of Scarborough or Brooklyn, the "Royal" or the "Grand"; their railways flank, plumb, and overhang a Hotel plucked from the history of the biggest, most ornate buildings in Italy, America, and Asia, whose windows and terraces are now brimming with lights, drinks, and heavy breezes, are wide open to souls of travelers and nobles alike—who permit, by day, the varied tarantellas of the shores—and even the ritornellos of art's storied valleys, to miraculously decorate the Promontory Palace facades.

DEVOTION

To my Sister Louise Vanaen de Voringhem: her blue habit turned towards the North Sea. —For the shipwrecked.

To my Sister Léonie Aubois d'Asby: *hooooo;* humming, stinking summer grass. —For fevers inflicting mothers and children.

To Lulu—that demon—who has retained a taste for oratories from the time of girlfriends and grammar school. For the Men! For Madame ★ ★ ★.

To the adolescent I was. To that holy old codger, hermitage or mission. To the spirit of the poor. And to an exalted clergy.

Just as to any cult, in any place that memorializes a cult, amid whatever events wherever we wander, subject to a moment's inspiration or the most serious vices.

Tonight, in the towering icy mirrors of Circeto, fat as fish, and illuminated like the ten months of the red night—(the fire of her amber heart)—my only prayer, as mute as these nocturnal regions, precedes gallantries more violent than this polar chaos.

At any price and in any place, even on metaphysical journeys.

—But no more *then.*

DEMOCRACY

"The flag fits the filthy land, and our argot drowns the drum.

"In cities, we nourish the most cynical prostitution. We slaughter logical revolts.

"To fragrant republics in flood! To serve the most monstrous military-industrial exploitations.

"Goodbye *here*, no matter where. Goodwill recruits, understand: our philosophy will be ferocity; ignorant of science, cads for comfort; to hell with the sputtering world. This road is real.

"Forward, march!"

STAGES

The comedy of old perpetuates itself while divvying up its idylls:

A street strewn with stages.

A long wooden pier running from one end of a rocky field to the other where barbarian hoards roam beneath bare trees.

Through corridors of black gauze following footsteps of passersby amidst lanterns and leaves.

Birds straight out of medieval mystery plays swoop down onto the masonry of floating stages stirred by a canopied archipelago of spectators' boats.

Lyrical scenes, accompanied by fife and drum, bow beneath nooks nestled near ceilings of lounges in modern clubs and oriental halls of yore.

The extravaganza moves to the top of an amphitheater crowned by a copse—or, instead, fidgets and warbles for the Boeotians, in the shadow of swaying trees on the fields' ridge.

On stage, the *opéra-comique* is divided at the intersection of ten partitions built between the gallery and the footlights.

HISTORIC EVENING

For example: an evening when a humble traveler withdraws from within earshot of impending economic doom, a master's hands may awaken a pastoral harpsichord; they play cards at the bottom of a pond, a mirror that conjures queens' and kings' favorites; there are saints, veils, threads of harmony, and chromatic strains at sunset.

He shudders at the approach of hunts and hordes. Comedy drips onto the grassy stage. Only then are the poor and weak ashamed, because of their stupid plans!

In his captive sight—Germany builds its way to the moon; Tatar deserts shine—old conflicts endure amidst a Celestial Empire; over stairways and armchairs of stone—a little world, pale and flat, Africa and Occident, rises. Then, a ballet of known nights and seas, a worthless chemistry, impossible melodies.

The same bourgeois magic wherever the mail train leaves us! The least sophisticated physicist feels it's no longer possible to endure this intimate atmosphere, a fog of physical remorse whose manifestation is disease enough.

No! The rise of heat, of sundered seas, of subterranean fires, of the planet's untethering and its resultant exterminations—facts from the Bible and the Nornes, presented without the least malice, and to which serious people will bear witness. —And yet, hardly the stuff of legend.

BOTTOM

Reality always too troublesome for my exalted character—I nonetheless found myself chez Madame, transformed into a big, blue-gray bird, soaring near the ceiling's moldings, trailing my wings through evening shadows.

At the foot of the baldachino that held her beloved jewels and bodily charms, I became a giant bear with purple gums and thick, miserable fur, eyes fixed on the crystal and silver on the sideboard.

Shadows swam, a torrid aquarium. In the morning—pugnacious June dawn—I ran to the fields, an ass, braying and brandishing my grief, until Sabines from the suburbs threw themselves upon my breast.

Bottom: Rimbaud's title for this poem was in English, as given.

H

Hortense's every gesture is violated by every atrocity. Her solitude, the mechanics of eroticism; her lassitude, the dynamics of love. Under childhood's watchful eye, she served, for countless years, as the fiery hygiene of races. Her door is open to misery. There, the morality of contemporary peoples is disembodied by her passion, or her action. —O the bitter shudder of young loves seen by gaslight on the bloody ground: Find Hortense!

MOVEMENT

The wagging movement along the banks of the river's falls,
The gulf at stern,
The slope's speed,
The current's pull
Flows through unimaginable lights
And new elements
Travelers enveloped in a valley of waterspouts
And *strom.*

These are the world's conquerors
Seeking their own elemental fortunes;
Sport and comfort travel with them;
They bring knowledge
Of race, classes, animals.
Aboard this Vessel.
Rest and restlessness
Under a flood of light
During terrible evenings of study.

Because from the banter around the instruments—blood, flowers, fire,
    jewels—
From the uneasy accountings aboard this fugitive craft,
We see, rolling like seawalls past a motorized hydraulic road:
Their monstrous store of studies, illuminated endlessly—
They are driven into harmonic ecstasy,
And heroics of discovery.
Beneath astonishing atmospheric accidents
A young couple remains alone on the ark
—Can ancient savageries be absolved?—
And sings, standing watch.

GENIUS

Because he has opened the house to foaming winter and to noisy summer, he is affection, he is now, he who purified what we drink, what we eat, he who is the charm of brief visits and the unearthly delight of destinations. He is affection, he is the future, strength, and love that we, standing in furious boredom, watch, passing through tempestuous skies, flying flags of ecstasy.

He is love, reinvented in perfect measure, reason both marvelous and unforeseen, and eternity: an instrument adored for its fatality. We have all known the terror of his sacrifice and of our own: Let us delight in our health, in the vigor of our faculties, in selfish affection and passion for him who loves us throughout his infinite days...

And we remember, and he embarks... And if Adoration goes away, and nonetheless rings, his promise rings: "Enough of these superstitions, these old bodies, these houses and days. Our time has fallen away!"

He will not depart, he will not descend from a heaven once again, he will not manage to redeem women's anger, and men's laughter, and all our sin: for it is already done, by his being, and being loved.

O his breaths, his faces, his flights; the terrible speed of formal perfection and action.

O fertile mind, boundless universe!

His body! Long-dreamt release and shattering grace meet new violence!

The sight of him, his sight! All old genuflections and sorrows are *lifted* in his wake.

His day! The abolition of all streaming, echoing sufferings through a music more intense.

His stride! Migration is more momentous than ancient invasions.

O he, and we! Old charities pale before such benevolent pride.

O world! And the clear song of new sorrows!

He knew us all and loved us all. This winter night, from cape to cape, from farthest pole to nearest château, from crowd to beach, from face to face, with weary emotions and waning strength, let us hail him, and see him, and send him forth, and down beneath the tides and up in snowy deserts, let us seek his sight, his breath, his body, his day.

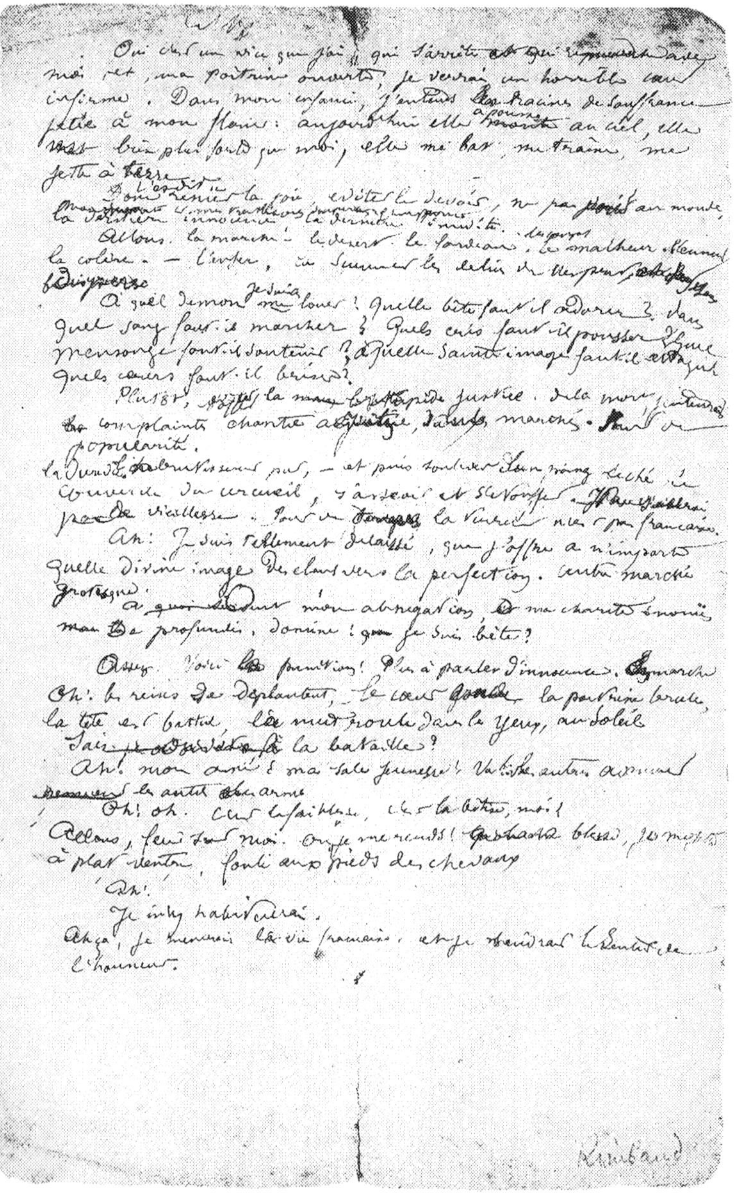

Oui c'est un vice que j'ai, qui s'arrête et qui reprend avec moi, et, ma poitrine ouverte, je verrais un horrible cœur infirme. Dans mon enfance, j'entends les racines de souffrance jetée à mon flanc : aujourd'hui elle a poussé au ciel, elle est bien plus forte que moi, elle me bat, me traîne, me jette à terre.

Donc renier la joie, éviter le devoir, ne pas porter au monde la dernière innocence, la dernière timidité.

Allons, la marche ! le désert, le fardeau, les coups, le malheur, l'ennui, la colère. — l'enfer, la science et les délices de l'esprit et des sens dispersés.

À quel démon je suis à louer ? Quelle bête faut-il adorer ? dans quel sang faut-il marcher ? Quels cris faut-il pousser ? Quel mensonge faut-il soutenir ? À quelle sainte image faut-il attaquer ? Quels cœurs faut-il briser ?

Plutôt, éviter la main brutale de la justice. De la mort, j'entends les complaintes chantées aujourd'hui, dans les marchés. Point de popularité.

La dure vie, l'abrutissement pur, — et puis soulever d'un poing séché le couvercle du cercueil, s'asseoir et s'étouffer. Je ne vieillirai pas de vieillesse. Point de dangers la terreur n'est pas française.

Ah ! je suis tellement délaissé, que j'offre à n'importe quelle divine image des élans vers la perfection. Autre marché grotesque.

À quoi servent mon abnégation et ma charité inouïes. mon De profundis, domine ! que je suis bête ?

Assez. Voici la punition ! Plus à parler d'innocence. En marche. Oh ! les reins se déplantent, le cœur gronde, la poitrine brûle, la tête est battue, la nuit roule dans les yeux, au soleil.

Sais-je où je vais ? À la bataille ?

Ah ! mon ami ! ma sale jeunesse ! Va..., va, les autres avancent les autels, les armes.

Oh ! oh. C'est la faiblesse, c'est la bêtise, moi !

Allons, feu sur moi. Ou je me rends ! Qu'on me blesse, je me jette à plat ventre, foulé aux pieds des chevaux.

Ah !

Je m'y habituerai.

Ah ça, je mènerais la vie française, et je suivrais le sentier de l'honneur.

Rimbaud

An early draft of Une saison en enfer.

A DRAFT OF *A SEASON IN HELL*

☙

The following fragmentary draft of A Season in Hell *was discovered in three pieces over the course of fifty years, beginning in 1897. Numerous transcriptions of the very fragile manuscript, which is difficult to read, exist. The translation is largely based on my collation of various transcriptions, principally those of Henri de Bouillane de Lacoste and Pierre Brunel, versions which differ considerably. Anything that appears within brackets is editorial conjecture. Interlineated text should be read as Rimbaud's alternatives to or replacements of the text immediately below it.*

[*FROM* BAD BLOOD]

Yes it's one of my vices, which stops and which ~~resumes~~ walks with me again, and, my chest open, I would see a horrible, sickly heart. During my childhood, I felt ~~the~~ its roots

grew

of suffering hurled at my side: today, it ~~climbs~~ to the sky, it ~~felt to me~~ is stronger than I am, it beats me, drags me, throws me to the ground.

it's said

So ^ renounce joy, avoid work, don't ~~play~~

my hope[?] and my higher treasons and my

in the world, ^the last innocence, the last timidity.

blows

We're off. March! the desert. the burden. ^ misfortune. boredom. anger.—hell, science and spiritual delight etc.

I'll fight for

Under ^ which demon's flag will I fight? What beast will I worship? through whose blood will I walk? What will I have to scream? What lies will I have to uphold? ~~At~~ what shrine will I have to attack which hearts have to break?

Better yet, ~~to avoid the bruta~~[l] ~~hand~~ to suffer[?] death's dumb justice, I will hear complaints sung ~~today, on the steps~~

the hard life

Justice endures[?]. Popular point. pure exhaustion—to lift the lid of the coffin with a withered fist, sit inside, and suffocate. ~~I won't grow old~~ No old age. Nor any dangers, terror isn't French.

Ah! I feel so forsaken, that I direct my instincts for perfection at any sacred image: another raw deal.

~~To what end~~ O my curtailment, ~~and~~ o my unbelievable charity ~~my~~ *De profunidis, domine!* ~~How~~ I am a fool?

Enough. Here's the punishment! No more talk of innocence. March Oh! My loins transplant themselves, the heart [illegible word], the chest burns, the head is battered, night rolls in the eyes, in the Sun ~~Do I know where, I go~~ Where will we fight?

Ah! My friend! My filthy youth! Go…go as the others advance ~~they move~~ altars and arms

Oh! Oh. It's weakness, foolishness, me!

Let's go, fire upon me or I'll give up! ~~The packsaddle~~ May someone wound me, I throw myself on my belly, trampled beneath the hooves of a horse.

Ah!

I'll get used to it.

Oh that, I would lead a French life, and I would follow the path of honor.

FALSE CONVERSION

Unhappy day! I swallowed a great ~~glass~~ gulp of poison. The rage of despair made me blow up against nature objects, me, which I would tear apart. May the advice I received be thrice blessed! ~~My~~ My gut burned the violence of the venom contorted by limbs, left me deformed. I die of thirst. I suffocate. I can't even cry out. This is hell eternal suffering. Look how ~~the~~ the flames rise! Demon, do your worst ~~devil,~~

> As one should
> It's
> a handsome and good

~~Satan~~ stir it up. I burn ~~well~~ ^ a good hell.

I once glimpsed ~~salvation~~ conversion, goodness, happiness, salvation. Can I even describe what I saw no one is a poet in hell ~~As soon as~~ it was ~~the apparition of thousands of charming people~~ an admirable spiritual song, strength and peace, noble ambitions, what else can I say!

Ah! noble ambitions! my hate. ~~I'll rebegin~~ Rebegin furious ~~The misfortune o my misfortune and the misfortune of others~~ which matters little to me existence: fury in the blood ~~animal life~~ the stupefaction ^ and its still life: if damnation is eternal. Its ~~still life still~~. The enactment of religious law why it was once sewn similarly in my spirit. ~~We had The~~ My parents caused my misfortune, and their own, which matters little to me. They took advantage of my innocence. Oh! The very idea of baptism. There are those who have lived badly, who live badly, and who feel nothing! It's my baptism and ~~the~~ my weakness to which I am a slave. Still alive! Later the delights of damnation will deepen. I recognize ~~the demon~~ damnation. ~~When~~ A man who wishes to

> I believe in hell so here I am

mutilate himself is assuredly damned. ^ Some crime, quick, so that I can fall into the void, in accordance with the law of man.

Shut up! Just shut up! This is all just shame and blame next to me; it's Satan who Satan himself says that his fire is lowly, idiotic, that my anger is horribly ugly.—Enough . . . ! Shut up! These are errors whispered in my ear ~~the~~ magics, ~~th~~

the.

alchemies, mysticisms, fake perfumes, childish music, Satan

So the poets are damned. No, that's not it.

takes care of all that.

And to think that I possess the truth. That I possess judgment both sound and sure on any subject, that I am prepared for perfection ~~Shut up, it's~~ pride! Now. I'm just a babe in the woods the skin on my scalp dries to dust. Pity! I am afraid, O Lord! my Lord! my lord. I am afraid, pity. Ah I'm thirsty, o my childhood, my village, the fields, the lake on the strand the moonlight when the clock strikes twelve. Satan is in the clock so that I'll go mad. O Mary, Holy Virgin false feeling, false prayer.

[*FROM* DELIRIA II: ALCHEMY OF THE WORD]

At last my spirit becomes[   ]
~~From London or Peking, or Ber~~[   ]
Which ~~disappear~~ we ~~joke on~~ [   ]
of general celebration. ~~Look~~ [   ]
the ~~little [illegible]~~ [   ]
I would have ~~wanted the chalky desert of~~ [   ]

I loved ward drinks, sunbleached shops, scorched orchards. I spent
many hours with my tongue hanging out, like an exhausted animal: I
dragged myself through the stinking streets, and eyes closed, I ~~prayed to~~
offered myself to the sun. God of fire, may he upend me, ~~and,~~ General,
king, I say, if you still have an old cannons [*sic*] on your collapsing ram-
parts, bombarding man with ~~pieces~~ lumps of dry earth. Strike splendid
shop mirrors! Cool sitting rooms! May ~~spiders And~~ [illegible word] Make
cities eat their dust! Coat gargoyles in
       quickly   burning boudoirs
rust. On time toss ruby sand the
~~I wore clothing made of~~ canvas. I [four illegible words] I broke stones
on roads forever swept clean. ~~The sun set towards the shit, at the center of~~
~~the earth~~ [three illegible words] a shit in
      convulsion
the valley a the drunken gnat in the urinal of an isolated inn,
                        dissolves in a sunbeam
smitten with the borage ~~and which will wilt in the sun~~

HUNGER

~~I think about~~ I thought about ~~about animals~~ the happiness of animals, caterpillars were the crowd [illegible word], ~~little~~

innocent

~~bodies~~ white bodies limbs: ~~the romantic spider made a romantic shadow invaded by the opal dawn~~; the brown bug

[illegible word]

person, waited ~~for us to~~ [illegible word] impassioned. Happy The mole, all virginity's sleep!

I withdrew ~~from contact~~ Shocking virginity, ~~which I try~~ to describe with a sort of romance Song from the tallest tower.

I believed I had found

~~I~~ [several illegible words, crossed out] reason and happiness. I listened ~~from~~ the sky, the blue, which is black, and I lived, a spark of gold struck from the *natural* light. It's very

I expressed ~~the most~~ stupidly.

serious.

ETERNITY

And ~~the crowning blow~~ Out of joy, I became a fabulous opera.

GOLDEN AGE

In this ~~period it was~~ it was my eternal life, unwritten, unsung,

worldly laws

—something like Providence in which one believes and which do not sing.

    After these noble minutes, ~~came~~ utter stupidity. I ~~myse~~ see a propensity for being undone by bliss in everyone: the action

not life   bad

wasn't but a ~~instinctive~~ means of wasting a belly full of life: ~~only, me I leave with the knowledge~~, a sweet and sinister risk, ~~an~~ disturbance, ~~deviation~~ bad habits. The moral ~~genius~~ was the weakness of the brain

[   ]beings and everything seemed to me

[   ]other lives around them. This monsieur

[   ]an angel. This family isn't

[   ]With many men

[   ]moment from one of their other lives

[   ]history no more principles. Nor another sophism of

I could repeat them all and others

imprisoned madness. I no longer felt a thing. The ~~hallucinations~~

and many others and others
I know how to do it

~~were~~ [several illegible crossed-out words] But now I would not try to make myself heard.

I believed

    A month of this. My sanity ~~fled~~ was threatened. I had more to do than merely live. The hallucinations were more alive ~~more~~

sadder and more remote

~~horrifying~~ the terror ~~no longer~~ came! I dreamt everywhere.

MEMORY

I found myself ripe for ~~demise~~, death and my weakness drew me to the edges of the earth and to a life where the whirlwind [...] in dark Cimmeria, country of the dead, where a great [...] took a dangerous route left nearly the whole soul with a [...] on a skiff coursed for dread.

ENDS OF THE EARTH

will shut my

I traveled a bit. I went North: I ~~will remember in~~ brain all

wanted to recognize the

the feudal odors, shepherdesses, primitive sources. I loved the sea [illegible phrase] ~~the magic ting in the luminous water illuminated~~ as if it was for her to wash me ~~clean of these aberrations~~ of a stain. I saw the consoling cross. I had been damned by the rainbow and religious; and thanks to Bliss,

magics

~~my remorse~~ my fate, my worm, and who ~~I~~ however ~~the world seems brand new, to me who had~~ raised every ~~the possible impressions~~; making my life too immense drained even after

only

my [illegible crossed-out word] to sincerely love strength and

very truly

beauty.

matutinum

In the biggest cities, at dawn, *ad diluculum,* when *Christus venit* ~~when for the strong among us Christ comes~~ her tooth, sweet as ~~the~~ death, warning me with the cock's crow.

---

ad diluculum: Dawn.

BL[IS]S

So weak I no longer thought society could bear my
                              Pity
                              Such misfortune
presence, except out of ^ What possible pasture for this beautiful disgust?
Benevol[ence].
    [Illegible phrase] Little by little it passed.
    Now I can't stand mystical leaps and stylistic strangenesses.
                              My beauty[?]
    Now I can say that art is folly. Our great poets just as easily: art is folly.
    Hail beauty.

Self-portrait, Rimbaud, c. 1883

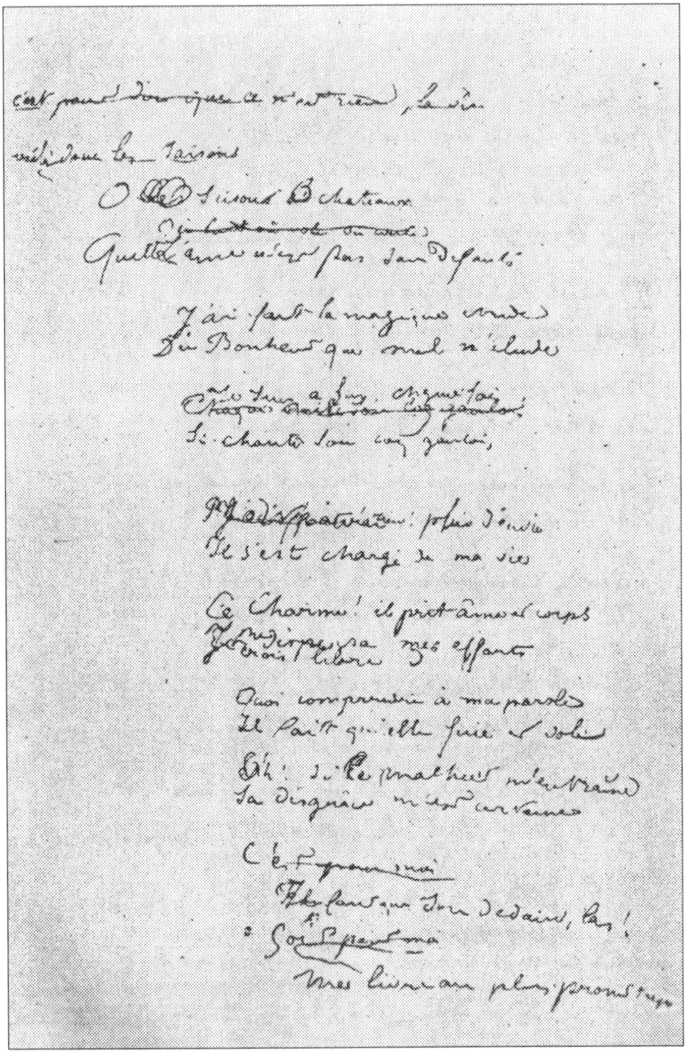

A draft of one version of "O saisons, o châteaux."

FOUR SEASONS

❧

Although multiple manuscript versions of many of Rimbaud's poems exist, in most instances the differences are illustrative of ambivalence over issues of capitalization or punctuation. The case of "O saisons, o châteaux" is very different, as the four versions we possess differ in substantial ways. They offer a partial view of Rimbaud leaping from an interesting, if messy, series of possibilities to a beautiful certainty, or certainties. The first two versions have never been translated into English before. The third is available everywhere, and the fourth is Rimbaud's final refinement printed in A Season in Hell.

In versions 1 and 2, my translations gloze the originals line by line. Version 3 is an alternate wording of the poem as it appears in Rimbaud Complete, *page 132. Version 4 is based on the French text of the poem as it appears* A Season in Hell; *however, the translation reproduced here differs considerably from the one on page 22. I reproduce these alternate solutions to offer a glimpse at the sorts of decisions faced by a translator of poetry.*

VERSION 1

~~c'est pour dire que ce n'est rien, la vie~~

~~voilà donc les saisons~~

~~which is to say that life is nothing~~

~~so here are the seasons~~

O les saisons et châteaux

~~Où court où vole où coule~~

L'âme n'est pas sans défauts

O the seasons and châteaux

~~Where runs where flies or flows~~

The soul isn't without flaws

J'ai fait la magique étude
Du Bonheur que nul n'élude

I made a magical study
Of Bliss, which no one escapes

~~Chaque [. . .] son coq gaulouis~~
Je suis à lui, chaque fois
Si chante son coq gaulois

~~Each [. . .] his Gallic cock~~
I follow him, every time
If his Gallic cock sings

~~Puis~~ J[. . .]rai rien: plus d'envie

~~Then~~ I [. . .] nothing: no more desire

Il s'est chargé de ma vie

It has taken control of my life

Ce Charme! il prit âme et corps
Et dispersa mes efforts

This charm! It takes soul and body
And disperses my efforts

Quoi comprendre à ma parole

What is to be understood from my words

Il fait qu'elle fuie et vole

The result is that they flee and fly

Eh! si le malheur m'entraîne
Sa disgrâce m'est certaine

If misfortune conditions me
My disgrace is assured at its hands

~~C'est pour moi~~
   Il faut que son dédain, las!
~~Soit pour moi~~
   Me livre ay plus prompt trép[as]

~~It's for me~~
   Alas his disdain
~~Either for me~~
   Delivers me directly to death[.]

VERSION 2

O saison O châteaux	O season O châteaux
Quelle L'âme n'est pas sans défauts	What The soul isn't without flaws
J'ai fait la magique étude	I made a magical study
Du Bonheur que nul n'élude	Of Bliss, which no one escapes
Je suis à lui, chaque fois	I follow him, every time
Si chante son coq gaulois	If his Gallic cock sings
[…] rien: plus d'envie	[…] nothing: no more desire
Il s'est chargé de ma vie	It has taken control of my life.
Ce Charme! il prit âme et corps	This charm! It takes soul and body
Je me crois libre d'efforts	I think I'm freed from exertions
Quoi comprendre à ma parole	What is to be understood from my words
Il fait qu'elle fuie et vole	The result is that they flee and fly
Oh! si ce malheur m'entraîne	Oh! If this misfortune conditions me
Sa disgrâce m'est certaine	My disgrace is assured at its hands
Il faut que son dédain, las!	Alas his disdain
Me livre au plus prompt trép[as]	Delivers me directly to death[.]

VERSION 3

O saisons, ô châteaux	O seasons, o châteaux
Quelle âme est sans défauts?	Who possesses a perfect soul?
O saisons, ô châteaux!	O seasons, o châteaux!
J'ai fait la magique étude	I made a magical study
Du Bonheur, que nul n'élude.	Of inescapable Bliss.
O vive lui, chaque fois	All hail Bliss, throughout Gaul
Que chante son coq Gaulois.	When you hear the rooster's call.
Mais! je n'aurai plus d'envie,	Bliss has finally set me free
Il s'est chargé de ma vie.	From desire's tyranny.
Ce Charme! il prit âme et corps.	Its spell took soul and shape,
Et dispersa tous efforts.	Letting every goal escape.
Que comprendre à ma parole?	What do my words mean?
Il fait qu'elle fuie et vole!	Meaning flees, takes wing!
o saisons, ô châteaux	o seasons, o châteaux

VERSION 4

O saisons, ô châteaux!
  Quelle âme est sans défauts?

J'ai fait la magique étude
Du bonheur, qu'aucun n'élude.

Salut à lui, chaque fois
Que chante le coq gaulois.

Ah! je n'aurai plus d'envie:
Il s'est chargé de ma vie.

Ce charme a pris âme et corps
Et dispersé les efforts.

  O saisons, ô châteaux!

L'heure de sa fuite, hélas!
Sera l'heure du trépas.

  O saisons, ô châteaux!

O seasons, o châteaux!
  Weakness visits every soul.

I made a magical exegesis
Of this Bliss that won't release us.

Think of Bliss each time you hear
The rooster's call, far or near.

I've been unburdened of desire:
Bliss is all I now require.

Its spell took shape and soul,
Eradicating every goal.

O seasons, o châteaux!

When Bliss departs at last
Death takes us each, alas.

O seasons, o châteaux!

FRENCH

A. RIMBAUD

UNE

SAISON EN ENFER

PRIX : UN FRANC

BRUXELLES

ALLIANCE TYPOGRAPHIQUE (M.-J. POOT ET COMPAGNIE)

37, rue aux Choux, 37

1873

****

Jadis, si je me souviens bien, ma vie était un festin où s'ouvraient tous les cœurs, où tous les vins coulaient.

Un soir, j'ai assis la Beauté sur mes genoux.—Et je l'ai trouvée amère.—Et je l'ai injuriée.

Je me suis armé contre la justice.

Je me suis enfui. Ô sorcières, ô misère, ô haine, c'est à vous que mon trésor a été confié!

Je parvins à faire s'évanouir dans mon esprit toute l'espérance humaine. Sur toute joie pour l'étrangler j'ai fait le bond sourd de la bête féroce.

J'ai appelé les bourreaux pour, en périssant, mordre la crosse de leurs fusils. J'ai appelé les fléaux, pour m'étouffer avec le sable, le sang. Le malheur a été mon dieu. Je me suis allongé dans la boue. Je me suis séché à l'air du crime. Et j'ai joué de bons tours à la folie.

Et le printemps m'a apporté l'affreux rire de l'idiot.

Or, tout dernièrement m'étant trouvé sur le point de faire le dernier *couac!* j'ai songé à rechercher la clef du festin ancien, où je reprendrais peut-être appétit.

La charité est cette clef.—Cette inspiration prouve que j'ai rêvé!

«Tu resteras hyène, etc...», se récrie le démon qui me couronna de si aimables pavots. «Gagne la mort avec tous tes appétits, et ton égoïsme et tous les péchés capitaux.»

Ah! j'en ai trop pris:—Mais, cher Satan, je vous en conjure, une prunelle moins irritée! et en attendant les quelques petites lâchetés en retard, vous qui aimez dans l'écrivain l'absence des facultés descriptives ou instructives, je vous détache ces quelques hideux feuillets de mon carnet de damné.

MAUVAIS SANG

J'ai de mes ancêtres gaulois l'œil bleu blanc, la cervelle étroite, et la maladresse dans la lutte. Je trouve mon habillement aussi barbare que le leur. Mais je ne beurre pas ma chevelure.

Les Gaulois étaient les écorcheurs de bêtes, les brûleurs d'herbes les plus ineptes de leur temps.

D'eux, j'ai: l'idolâtrie et l'amour du sacrilège;—oh! tous les vices, colère, luxure,—magnifique, la luxure;—surtout mensonge et paresse.

J'ai horreur de tous les métiers. Maîtres et ouvriers, tous paysans, ignobles. La main à plume vaut la main à charrue.—Quel siècle à mains!—Je n'aurai jamais ma main. Après, la domesticité mène trop loin. L'honnêteté de la mendicité me navre. Les criminels dégoûtent comme des châtrés: moi, je suis intact, et ça m'est égal.

Mais! qui a fait ma langue perfide tellement, qu'elle ait guidé et sauve-gardé jusqu'ici ma paresse? Sans me servir pour vivre même de mon corps, et plus oisif que le crapaud, j'ai vécu partout. Pas une famille d'Europe que je ne connaisse.—J'entends des familles comme la mienne, qui tiennent tout de la déclaration des Droits de l'Homme.—J'ai connu chaque fils de famille!

———

Si j'avais des antécédents à un point quelconque de l'histoire de France! Mais non, rien.

Il m'est bien évident que j'ai toujours été race inférieure. Je ne puis comprendre la révolte. Ma race ne se souleva jamais que pour piller: tels les loups à la bête qu'ils n'ont pas tuée.

Je me rappelle l'histoire de la France fille aînée de l'Église. J'aurais fait, manant, le voyage de terre sainte; j'ai dans la tête des routes dans les plaines souabes, des vues de Byzance, des remparts de Solyme; le culte de Marie, l'attendrissement sur le crucifié s'éveillent en moi parmi mille féeries profanes.—Je suis assis, lépreux, sur les pots cassés et les orties, au pied d'un mur rongé par le soleil.—Plus tard, reître, j'aurais bivaqué sous les nuits d'Allemagne.

Ah! encore: je danse le sabbat dans une rouge clairière, avec des vieilles et des enfants.

Je ne me souviens pas plus loin que cette terre-ci et le christianisme. Je n'en finirais pas de me revoir dans ce passé. Mais toujours seul; sans famille; même, quelle langue parlais-je? Je ne me vois jamais dans les conseils du Christ; ni dans les conseils des Seigneurs,—représentants du Christ.

Qu'étais-je au siècle dernier: je ne me retrouve qu'aujourd'hui. Plus de vagabonds, plus de guerres vagues. La race inférieure a tout couvert—le peuple, comme on dit, la raison; la nation et la science.

Oh! la science! On a tout repris. Pour le corps et pour l'âme,—le viatique,—on a la médecine et la philosophie,—les remèdes de bonnes femmes et les chansons populaires arrangées. Et les divertissements des princes et les jeux qu'ils interdisaient! Géographie, cosmographie, mécanique, chimie!...

La science, la nouvelle noblesse! Le progrès. Le monde marche! Pourquoi ne tournerait-il pas?

C'est la vision des nombres. Nous allons à l'*Esprit*. C'est très-certain, c'est oracle, ce que je dis. Je comprends, et ne sachant m'expliquer sans paroles païennes, je voudrais me taire.

———

Le sang païen revient! L'Esprit est proche, pourquoi Christ ne m'aide-t-il pas, en donnant à mon âme noblesse et liberté. Hélas! l'Évangile a passé! l'Évangile! l'Évangile.

J'attends Dieu avec gourmandise. Je suis de race inférieure de toute éternité.

Me voici sur la plage armoricaine. Que les villes s'allument dans le soir. Ma journée est faite; je quitte l'Europe. L'air marin brûlera mes poumons; les climats perdus me tanneront. Nager, broyer l'herbe, chasser, fumer surtout; boire des liqueurs fortes comme du métal bouillant,—comme faisaient ces chers ancêtres autour des feux.

Je reviendrai, avec des membres de fer, la peau sombre, l'œil furieux: sur mon masque, on me jugera d'une race forte. J'aurai de l'or: je serai oisif et brutal. Les femmes soignent ces féroces infirmes retour des pays chauds. Je serai mêlé aux affaires politiques. Sauvé.

Maintenant je suis maudit, j'ai horreur de la patrie. Le meilleur, c'est un sommeil bien ivre, sur la grève.

———

On ne part pas.—Reprenons les chemins d'ici, chargé de mon vice, le vice qui a poussé ses racines de souffrance à mon côté, dès l'âge de raison—qui monte au ciel, me bat, me renverse, me traîne.

La dernière innocence et la dernière timidité. C'est dit. Ne pas porter au monde mes dégoûts et mes trahisons.

Allons! La marche, le fardeau, le désert, l'ennui et la colère.

À qui me louer? Quelle bête faut-il adorer? Quelle sainte image attaque-t-on? Quels cœurs briserai-je? Quel mensonge dois-je tenir?— Dans quel sang marcher?

Plutôt, se garder de la justice.—La vie dure, l'abrutissement simple,— soulever, le poing desséché, le couvercle du cercueil, s'asseoir, s'étouffer. Ainsi point de vieillesse, ni de dangers: la terreur n'est pas française.

—Ah! je suis tellement délaissé que j'offre à n'importe quelle divine image des élans vers la perfection.

Ô mon abnégation, ô ma charité merveilleuse! ici-bas, pourtant!

De profundis Domine, suis-je bête!

———

Encore tout enfant, j'admirais le forçat intraitable sur qui se referme toujours le bagne; je visitais les auberges et les garnis qu'il aurait sacrés par son séjour; je voyais *avec son idée* le ciel bleu et le travail fleuri de la campagne; je flairais sa fatalité dans les villes. Il avait plus de force qu'un saint, plus de bon sens qu'un voyageur—et lui, lui seul! pour témoin de sa gloire et de sa raison.

Sur les routes, par des nuits d'hiver, sans gîte, sans habits, sans pain, une voix étreignait mon cœur gelé: «Faiblesse ou force: te voilà, c'est la force. Tu ne sais ni où tu vas ni pourquoi tu vas, entre partout, réponds à tout. On ne te tuera pas plus que si tu étais cadavre.» Au matin j'avais le regard si perdu et la contenance si morte, que ceux que j'ai rencontrés *ne m'ont peut-être pas vu.*

Dans les villes la boue m'apparaissait soudainement rouge et noire, comme une glace quand la lampe circule dans la chambre voisine, comme un trésor dans la forêt! Bonne chance, criais-je, et je voyais une mer de flammes et de fumée au ciel; et, à gauche, à droite, toutes les richesses flambant comme un milliard de tonnerres.

Mais l'orgie et la camaraderie des femmes m'étaient interdites. Pas même un compagnon. Je me voyais devant une foule exaspérée, en face du peloton d'exécution, pleurant du malheur qu'ils n'aient pu comprendre, et pardonnant!—Comme Jeanne d'Arc!—«Prêtres, professeurs, maîtres, vous vous trompez en me livrant à la justice. Je n'ai jamais été de ce peuple-ci; je n'ai jamais été chrétien; je suis de la race qui chantait dans le supplice; je ne comprends pas les lois; je n'ai pas le sens moral, je suis une brute: vous vous trompez...»

Oui, j'ai les yeux fermés à votre lumière. Je suis une bête, un nègre. Mais je puis être sauvé. Vous êtes de faux nègres, vous maniaques, féroces, avares. Marchand, tu es nègre; magistrat, tu es nègre; général, tu es nègre; empereur, vieille démangeaison, tu es nègre: tu as bu d'une liqueur non taxée, de la fabrique de Satan.—Ce peuple est inspiré par la fièvre et le cancer. Infirmes et vieillards sont tellement respectables qu'ils demandent à être bouillis.—Le plus malin est de quitter ce continent, où la folie rôde pour pourvoir d'otages ces misérables. J'entre au vrai royaume des enfants de Cham.

Connais-je encore la nature? me connais-je?—*Plus de mots.* J'ensevelis les morts dans mon ventre. Cris, tambour, danse, danse, danse, danse! Je ne vois même pas l'heure où, les blancs débarquant, je tomberai au néant.

Faim, soif, cris, danse, danse, danse, danse!

———

Les blancs débarquent. Le canon! Il faut se soumettre au baptême, s'habiller, travailler.

J'ai reçu au cœur le coup de la grâce. Ah! je ne l'avais pas prévu!

Je n'ai point fait le mal. Les jours vont m'être légers, le repentir me sera épargné. Je n'aurai pas eu les tourments de l'âme presque morte au bien, où remonte la lumière sévère comme les cierges funéraires. Le sort du fils de famille, cercueil prématuré couvert de limpides larmes. Sans doute la débauche est bête, le vice est bête; il faut jeter la pourriture à l'écart. Mais l'horloge ne sera pas arrivée à ne plus sonner que l'heure de la pure douleur! Vais-je être enlevé comme un enfant, pour jouer au paradis dans l'oubli de tout le malheur!

Vite! est-il d'autres vies?—Le sommeil dans la richesse est impossible. La richesse a toujours été bien public. L'amour divin seul octroie les clefs de la science. Je vois que la nature n'est qu'un spectacle de bonté. Adieu chimères, idéals, erreurs.

Le chant raisonnable des anges s'élève du navire sauveur: c'est l'amour divin.—Deux amours! je puis mourir de l'amour terrestre, mourir de dévouement. J'ai laissé des âmes dont la peine s'accroîtra de mon départ! Vous me choisissez parmi les naufragés; ceux qui restent sont-ils pas mes amis?

Sauvez-les!

La raison m'est née. Le monde est bon. Je bénirai la vie. J'aimerai mes frères. Ce ne sont plus des promesses d'enfance. Ni l'espoir d'échapper à la vieillesse et à la mort. Dieu fait ma force, et je loue Dieu.

————

L'ennui n'est plus mon amour. Les rages, les débauches, la folie, dont je sais tous les élans et les désastres,—tout mon fardeau est déposé. Apprécions sans vertige l'étendue de mon innocence.

Je ne serais plus capable de demander le réconfort d'une bastonnade. Je ne me crois pas embarqué pour une noce avec Jésus-Christ pour beau-père.

Je ne suis pas prisonnier de ma raison. J'ai dit: Dieu. Je veux la liberté dans le salut: comment la poursuivre? Les goûts frivoles m'ont quitté. Plus besoin de dévouement ni d'amour divin. Je ne regrette pas le siècle des cœurs sensibles. Chacun a sa raison, mépris et charité: je retiens ma place au sommet de cette angélique échelle de bon sens.

Quant au bonheur établi, domestique ou non... non, je ne peux pas. Je suis trop dissipé, trop faible. La vie fleurit par le travail, vieille vérité: moi, ma vie n'est pas assez pesante, elle s'envole et flotte loin au-dessus de l'action, ce cher point du monde.

Comme je deviens vieille fille, à manquer du courage d'aimer la mort!

Si Dieu m'accordait le calme céleste, aérien, la prière,—comme les anciens saints.—Les saints! des forts! les anachorètes, des artistes comme il n'en faut plus!

Farce continuelle! Mon innocence me ferait pleurer. La vie est la farce à mener par tous.

———

Assez! voici la punition.—*En marche!*

Ah! les poumons brûlent, les tempes grondent! la nuit roule dans mes yeux, par ce soleil! le cœur... les membres...

Où va-t-on? au combat? Je suis faible! les autres avancent. Les outils, les armes... le temps!...

Feu! feu sur moi! Là! ou je me rends.—Lâches!—Je me tue! Je me jette aux pieds des chevaux!

Ah!...

—Je m'y habituerai.

Ce serait la vie française, le sentier de l'honneur!

NUIT DE L'ENFER

J'ai avalé une fameuse gorgée de poison.—Trois fois béni soit le conseil qui m'est arrivé!—Les entrailles me brûlent. La violence du venin tord mes membres, me rend difforme, me terrasse. Je meurs de soif, j'étouffe, je ne puis crier. C'est l'enfer, l'éternelle peine! Voyez comme le feu se relève! Je brûle comme il faut. Va, démon!

J'avais entrevu la conversion au bien et au bonheur, le salut. Puis-je décrire la vision, l'air de l'enfer ne souffre pas les hymnes! C'était des millions de créatures charmantes, un suave concert spirituel, la force et la paix, les nobles ambitions, que sais-je?

Les nobles ambitions!

Et c'est encore la vie!—Si la damnation est éternelle! Un homme qui veut se mutiler est bien damné, n'est-ce pas? Je me crois en enfer, donc j'y suis. C'est l'exécution du catéchisme. Je suis esclave de mon baptême. Parents, vous avez fait mon malheur et vous avez fait le vôtre. Pauvre innocent!—L'enfer ne peut attaquer les païens.—C'est la vie encore! Plus tard, les délices de la damnation seront plus profondes. Un crime, vite, que je tombe au néant, de par la loi humaine.

Tais-toi, mais tais-toi!... C'est la honte, le reproche, ici: Satan qui dit que le feu est ignoble, que ma colère est affreusement sotte.— Assez!... Des erreurs qu'on me souffle, magies, parfums faux, musiques puériles.—Et dire que je tiens la vérité, que je vois la justice: j'ai un jugement sain et arrêté, je suis prêt pour la perfection... Orgueil.—La peau de ma tête se dessèche. Pitié! Seigneur, j'ai peur. J'ai soif, si soif! Ah! l'enfance, l'herbe, la pluie, le lac sur les pierres, *le clair de lune quand le clocher sonnait douze*... le diable est au clocher, à cette heure. Marie! Sainte-Vierge!... —Horreur de ma bêtise.

Là-bas, ne sont-ce pas des âmes honnêtes, qui me veulent du bien... Venez... J'ai un oreiller sur la bouche, elles ne m'entendent pas, ce sont des fantômes. Puis, jamais personne ne pense à autrui. Qu'on n'approche pas. Je sens le roussi, c'est certain.

Les hallucinations sont innombrables. C'est bien ce que j'ai toujours eu: plus de foi en l'histoire, l'oubli des principes. Je m'en tairai: poètes et visionnaires seraient jaloux. Je suis mille fois le plus riche, soyons avare comme la mer.

Ah çà! l'horloge de la vie s'est arrêtée tout à l'heure. Je ne suis plus au monde.—La théologie est sérieuse, l'enfer est certainement *en bas*—et le ciel en haut.—Extase, cauchemar, sommeil dans un nid de flammes.

Que de malices dans l'attention dans la campagne...Satan, Ferdinand, court avec les graines sauvages...Jésus marche sur les ronces purpurines, sans les courber...Jésus marchait sur les eaux irritées. La lanterne nous le montra debout, blanc et des tresses brunes, au flanc d'une vague d'émeraude...

Je vais dévoiler tous les mystères: mystères religieux ou naturels, mort, naissance, avenir, passé, cosmogonie, néant. Je suis maître en fantasmagories.

Écoutez!...

J'ai tous les talents!—Il n'y a personne ici et il y a quelqu'un: je ne voudrais pas répandre mon trésor.—Veut-on des chants nègres, des danses de houris? Veut-on que je disparaisse, que je plonge à la recherche de l'*anneau*? Veut-on? Je ferai de l'or, des remèdes.

Fiez-vous donc à moi, la foi soulage, guide, guérit. Tous, venez,—même les petits enfants,—que je vous console, qu'on répande pour vous son cœur,—le cœur merveilleux!—Pauvres hommes, travailleurs! Je ne demande pas de prières; avec votre confiance seulement, je serai heureux.

—Et pensons à moi. Ceci me fait peu regretter le monde. J'ai de la chance de ne pas souffrir plus. Ma vie ne fut que folies douces, c'est regrettable.

Bah! faisons toutes les grimaces imaginables.

Décidément, nous sommes hors du monde. Plus aucun son. Mon tact a disparu. Ah! mon château, ma Saxe, mon bois de saules. Les soirs, les matins, les nuits, les jours...Suis-je las!

Je devrais avoir mon enfer pour la colère, mon enfer pour l'orgueil,—et l'enfer de la caresse; un concert d'enfers.

Je meurs de lassitude. C'est le tombeau, je m'en vais aux vers, horreur de l'horreur! Satan, farceur, tu veux me dissoudre, avec tes charmes. Je réclame. Je réclame! un coup de fourche, une goutte de feu.

Ah! remonter à la vie! Jeter les yeux sur nos difformités. Et ce poison, ce baiser mille fois maudit! Ma faiblesse, la cruauté du monde! Mon Dieu, pitié, cachez-moi, je me tiens trop mal!—Je suis caché et je ne le suis pas.

C'est le feu qui se relève avec son damné.

DÉLIRES

I

L'ÉPOUX INFERNAL
Vierge folle

Écoutons la confession d'un compagnon d'enfer:

«Ô divin Époux, mon Seigneur, ne refusez pas la confession de la plus triste de vos servantes. Je suis perdue. Je suis soûle. Je suis impure. Quelle vie!

«Pardon, divin Seigneur, pardon! Ah! pardon! Que de larmes! Et que de larmes encore plus tard, j'espère!

«Plus tard, je connaîtrai le divin Époux! Je suis née soumise à Lui.—L'autre peut me battre maintenant!

«À présent, je suis au fond du monde! Ô mes amies!...non, pas mes amies...Jamais délires ni tortures semblables...Est-ce bête!

«Ah! je souffre, je crie. Je souffre vraiment. Tout pourtant m'est permis, chargée du mépris des plus méprisables cœurs.

«Enfin, faisons cette confidence, quitte à la répéter vingt autres fois,—aussi morne, aussi insignifiante!

«Je suis esclave de l'Époux infernal, celui qui a perdu les vierges folles. C'est bien ce démon-là. Ce n'est pas un spectre, ce n'est pas un fantôme. Mais moi qui ai perdu la sagesse, qui suis damnée et morte au monde,—on ne me tuera pas!—Comment vous le décrire! Je ne sais même plus parler. Je suis en deuil, je pleure, j'ai peur. Un peu de fraîcheur, Seigneur, si vous voulez, si vous voulez bien!

«Je suis veuve...—J'étais veuve...—mais oui, j'ai été bien sérieuse jadis, et je ne suis pas née pour devenir squelette!...—Lui était presque un enfant...Ses délicatesses mystérieuses m'avaient séduite. J'ai oublié tout mon devoir humain pour le suivre. Quelle vie! La vraie vie est absente. Nous ne sommes pas au monde. Je vais où il va, il le faut. Et souvent il s'emporte contre moi, *moi, la pauvre âme*. Le Démon!—C'est un Démon, vous savez, *ce n'est pas un homme.*

«Il dit: "Je n'aime pas les femmes. L'amour est à réinventer, on le sait. Elles ne peuvent plus que vouloir une position assurée. La position gagnée, cœur et beauté sont mis de côté: il ne reste que froid dédain, l'aliment du mariage, aujourd'hui. Ou bien je vois des femmes, avec les signes du bonheur, dont, moi, j'aurais pu faire de bonnes camarades, dévorées tout d'abord par des brutes sensibles comme des bûchers…"

«Je l'écoute faisant de l'infamie une gloire, de la cruauté un charme. "Je suis de race lointaine: mes pères étaient Scandinaves: ils se perçaient les côtes, buvaient leur sang.—Je me ferai des entailles partout le corps, je me tatouerai, je veux devenir hideux comme un Mongol: tu verras, je hurlerai dans les rues. Je veux devenir bien fou de rage. Ne me montre jamais de bijoux, je ramperais et me tordrais sur le tapis. Ma richesse, je la voudrais tachée de sang partout. Jamais je ne travaillerai…" Plusieurs nuits, son démon me saisissant, nous nous roulions, je luttais avec lui!— Les nuits, souvent, ivre, il se poste dans des rues ou dans des maisons, pour m'épouvanter mortellement.—"On me coupera vraiment le cou; ce sera dégoûtant." Oh! ces jours où il veut marcher avec l'air du crime!

«Parfois il parle, en une façon de patois attendri, de la mort qui fait repentir, des malheureux qui existent certainement, des travaux pénibles, des départs qui déchirent les cœurs. Dans les bouges où nous nous enivrions, il pleurait en considérant ceux qui nous entouraient, bétail de la misère. Il relevait les ivrognes dans les rues noires. Il avait la pitié d'une mère méchante pour les petits enfants.—Il s'en allait avec des gentillesses de petite fille au catéchisme.—Il feignait d'être éclairé sur tout, commerce, art, médecine.—Je le suivais, il le faut!

«Je voyais tout le décor dont, en esprit, il s'entourait; vêtements, draps, meubles: je lui prêtais des armes, une autre figure. Je voyais tout ce qui le touchait, comme il aurait voulu le créer pour lui. Quand il me semblait avoir l'esprit inerte, je le suivais, moi, dans des actions étranges et compliquées, loin, bonnes ou mauvaises: j'étais sûre de ne jamais entrer dans son monde. À côté de son cher corps endormi, que d'heures des nuits j'ai veillé, cherchant pourquoi il voulait tant s'évader de la réalité. Jamais homme n'eut pareil vœu. Je reconnaissais,—sans craindre pour lui,— qu'il pouvait être un sérieux danger dans la société.—Il a peut-être des secrets pour *changer la vie?* Non, il ne fait qu'en chercher, me répliquais-je. Enfin sa charité est ensorcelée, et j'en suis la prisonnière. Aucune autre âme n'aurait assez de force,—force de désespoir!—pour la supporter,—pour être protégée et aimée par lui. D'ailleurs, je ne me le figurais pas avec une autre âme: on voit son Ange, jamais l'Ange d'un autre,—je crois. J'étais dans son âme comme dans un palais qu'on a vidé pour ne pas voir une personne si peu noble que vous: voilà tout. Hélas! je dépendais bien de lui. Mais que voulait-il avec mon existence terne et lâche? Il ne me rendait pas meilleure, s'il ne me faisait pas mourir! Tristement dépitée, je lui dis quelquefois: "Je te comprends." Il haussait les épaules.

«Ainsi, mon chagrin se renouvelant sans cesse, et me trouvant plus égarée à mes yeux,—comme à tous les yeux qui auraient voulu me fixer, si je n'eusse été condamnée pour jamais à l'oubli de tous!—j'avais de plus en plus faim de sa bonté. Avec ses baisers et ses étreintes amies, c'était bien un ciel, un sombre ciel, où j'entrais, et où j'aurais voulu être laissée, pauvre, sourde, muette, aveugle. Déjà j'en prenais l'habitude. Je nous voyais comme deux bons enfants, libres de se promener dans le Paradis de tristesse. Nous nous accordions. Bien émus, nous travaillions ensemble. Mais, après une pénétrante caresse, il disait: "Comme ça te paraîtra drôle, quand je n'y serai plus, ce par quoi tu as passé. Quand tu n'auras plus mes bras sous ton cou, ni mon cœur pour t'y reposer, ni cette bouche sur tes yeux. Parce qu'il faudra que je m'en aille, très loin, un jour. Puis il faut que j'en aide d'autres: c'est mon devoir. Quoique ce ne soit guère ragoûtant…, chère âme…" Tout de suite je me pressentais, lui parti, en proie au vertige, précipitée dans l'ombre la plus affreuse: la mort. Je lui faisais promettre qu'il ne me lâcherait pas. Il l'a faite vingt fois, cette promesse d'amant. C'était aussi frivole que moi lui disant: "Je te comprends."

«Ah! je n'ai jamais été jalouse de lui. Il ne me quittera pas, je crois. Que devenir? Il n'a pas une connaissance, il ne travaillera jamais. Il veut vivre somnambule. Seules, sa bonté et sa charité lui donneraient-elles droit dans le monde réel? Par instants, j'oublie la pitié où je suis tombée: lui me rendra forte, nous voyagerons, nous chasserons dans les déserts, nous dormirons sur les pavés des villes inconnues, sans soins, sans peines. Ou je me réveillerai, et les lois et les mœurs auront changé,—grâce à son pouvoir magique,—le monde, en restant le même, me laissera à mes désirs, joies, nonchalances. Oh! la vie d'aventures qui existe dans les livres des enfants, pour me récompenser, j'ai tant souffert, me la donneras-tu? Il ne peut pas. J'ignore son idéal. Il m'a dit avoir des regrets, des espoirs: cela ne doit pas me regarder. Parle-t-il à Dieu? Peut-être devrais-je m'adresser à Dieu. Je suis au plus profond de l'abîme, et je ne sais plus prier.

«S'il m'expliquait ses tristesses, les comprendrais-je plus que ses railleries? Il m'attaque, il passe des heures à me faire honte de tout ce qui m'a pu toucher au monde, et s'indigne si je pleure.

«"Tu vois cet élégant jeune homme, entrant dans la belle et calme maison: il s'appelle Duval, Dufour, Armand, Maurice, que sais-je? Une femme s'est dévouée à aimer ce méchant idiot: elle est morte, c'est certes une sainte au ciel, à présent. Tu me feras mourir comme il a fait mourir cette femme. C'est notre sort, à nous, cœurs charitables…" Hélas! il avait des jours où tous les hommes agissant lui paraissaient les jouets de délires grotesques: il riait affreusement, longtemps.—Puis, il reprenait ses manières de jeune mère, de sœur aimée. S'il était moins sauvage, nous serions sauvés! Mais sa douceur aussi est mortelle. Je lui suis soumise.—Ah! je suis folle!

«Un jour peut-être il disparaîtra merveilleusement; mais il faut que je sache, s'il doit remonter à un ciel, que je voie un peu l'assomption de mon petit ami!»

Drôle de ménage!

DÉLIRES

II
Alchimie du verbe

À moi. L'histoire d'une de mes folies.

Depuis longtemps je me vantais de posséder tous les paysages possibles, et trouvais dérisoires les célébrités de la peinture et de la poésie moderne.

J'aimais les peintures idiotes, dessus de portes, décors, toiles de saltimbanques, enseignes, enluminures populaires; la littérature démodée, latin d'église, livres érotiques sans orthographe, romans de nos aïeules, contes de fées, petits livres de l'enfance, opéras vieux, refrains niais, rhythmes naïfs.

Je rêvais croisades, voyages de découvertes dont on n'a pas de relations, républiques sans histoires, guerres de religion étouffées, révolutions de mœurs, déplacements de races et de continents: je croyais à tous les enchantements.

J'inventai la couleur des voyelles!—*A* noir, *E* blanc, *I* rouge, *O* bleu, *U* vert.—Je réglai la forme et le mouvement de chaque consonne, et, avec des rhythmes instinctifs, je me flattai d'inventer un verbe poétique accessible, un jour ou l'autre, à tous les sens. Je réservais la traduction.

Ce fut d'abord une étude. J'écrivais des silences, des nuits, je notais l'inexprimable. Je fixais des vertiges.

———

> Loin des oiseaux, des troupeaux, des villageoises,
> Que buvais-je, à genoux dans cette bruyère
> Entourée de tendres bois de noisetiers,
> Dans un brouillard d'après-midi tiède et vert?
>
> Que pouvais-je boire dans cette jeune Oise,
> —Ormeaux sans voix, gazon sans fleurs, ciel couvert!—

Boire à ces gourdes jaunes, loin de ma case
Chérie? Quelque liqueur d'or qui fait suer.

Je faisais une louche enseigne d'auberge.
—Un orage vint chasser le ciel. Au soir
L'eau des bois se perdait sur les sables vierges,
Le vent de Dieu jetait des glaçons aux mares;

Pleurant, je voyais de l'or—et ne pus boire.—

———

À quatre heures du matin, l'été,
Le sommeil d'amour dure encore.
Sous les bocages s'évapore
    L'odeur du soir fêté.

Là-bas, dans leur vaste chantier
Au soleil des Hespérides,
Déjà s'agitent—en bras de chemise—
    Les Charpentiers.

Dans leurs Déserts de mousse, tranquilles,
Ils préparent les lambris précieux
Où la ville
    Peindra de faux cieux.

Ô, pour ces Ouvriers charmants
Sujets d'un roi de Babylone,
Vénus! quitte un instant les Amants
    Dont l'âme est en couronne.

Ô Reine des Bergers,
Porte aux travailleurs l'eau-de-vie,
Que leurs forces soient en paix
En attendant le bain dans la mer à midi.

La vieillerie poétique avait une bonne part dans mon alchimie du verbe.

Je m'habituai à l'hallucination simple: je voyais très-franchement une mosquée à la place d'une usine, une école de tambours faite par des anges, des calèches sur les routes du ciel, un salon au fond d'un lac; les monstres, les mystères; un titre de vaudeville dressait des épouvantes devant moi.

Puis j'expliquai mes sophismes magiques avec l'hallucination des mots!

Je finis par trouver sacré le désordre de mon esprit. J'étais oisif, en proie à une lourde fièvre: j'enviais la félicité des bêtes,—les chenilles, qui représentent l'innocence des limbes, les taupes, le sommeil de la virginité!

Mon caractère s'aigrissait. Je disais adieu au monde dans d'espèces de romances:

CHANSON DE LA PLUS HAUTE TOUR

> Qu'il vienne, qu'il vienne,
> Le temps dont on s'éprenne.

> J'ai tant fait patience
> Qu'à jamais j'oublie.
> Craintes et souffrances
> Aux cieux sont parties.
> Et la soif malsaine
> Obscurcit mes veines.

> Qu'il vienne, qu'il vienne,
> Le temps dont on s'éprenne.

> Telle la prairie
> À l'oubli livrée,

Grandie, et fleurie
D'encens et d'ivraies,
Au bourdon farouche
Des sales mouches.

Qu'il vienne, qu'il vienne,
Le temps dont on s'éprenne.

J'aimai le désert, les vergers brûlés, les boutiques fanées, les boissons tiédies. Je me traînais dans les ruelles puantes et, les yeux fermés, je m'offrais au soleil, dieu de feu.

«Général, s'il reste un vieux canon sur tes remparts en ruines, bombarde-nous avec des blocs de terre sèche. Aux glaces des magasins splendides! dans les salons! Fais manger sa poussière à la ville. Oxyde les gargouilles. Emplis les boudoirs de poudre de rubis brûlante...»

Oh! le moucheron enivré à la pissotière de l'auberge, amoureux de la bourrache, et que dissout un rayon!

FAIM

Si j'ai du goût, ce n'est guère
Que pour la terre et les pierres.
Je déjeune toujours d'air,
De roc, de charbons, de fer.

Mes faims, tournez. Paissez, faims,
Le pré des sons.
Attirez le gai venin
Des liserons.

Mangez les cailloux qu'on brise,
Les vieilles pierres d'églises;
Les galets des vieux déluges,
Pains semés dans les vallées grises.

―――――

Le loup criait sous les feuilles
En crachant les belles plumes
De son repas de volailles:
Comme lui je me consume.

Les salades, les fruits
N'attendent que la cueillette;
Mais l'araignée de la haie
Ne mange que des violettes.

Que je dorme! que je bouille
Aux autels de Salomon.
Le bouillon court sur la rouille,
Et se mêle au Cédron.

Enfin, ô bonheur, ô raison, j'écartai du ciel l'azur, qui est du noir, et je
vécus, étincelle d'or de la lumière *nature*. De joie, je prenais une expres-
sion bouffonne et égarée au possible:

Elle est retrouvée!
Quoi? l'éternité.
C'est la mer mêlée
            Au soleil.

Mon âme éternelle,
Observe ton vœu
Malgré la nuit seule
Et le jour en feu.

Donc tu te dégages
Des humains suffrages,
Des communs élans!
Tu voles selon…

—Jamais l'espérance.
                    Pas d'*orietur.*
Science et patience,
Le supplice est sûr.

Plus de lendemain,
Braises de satin,
                    Votre ardeur
                    Est le devoir.

Elle est retrouvée!
—Quoi?—l'Éternité.
C'est la mer mêlée
                    Au soleil.

————

Je devins un opéra fabuleux: je vis que tous les êtres ont une fatalité de bonheur: l'action n'est pas la vie, mais une façon de gâcher quelque force, un énervement. La morale est la faiblesse de la cervelle.

À chaque être, plusieurs *autres* vies me semblaient dues. Ce monsieur ne sait ce qu'il fait: il est un ange. Cette famille est une nichée de chiens. Devant plusieurs hommes, je causai tout haut avec un moment d'une de leurs autres vies.—Ainsi, j'ai aimé un porc.

Aucun des sophismes de la folie,—la folie qu'on enferme,—n'a été oublié par moi: je pourrais les redire tous, je tiens le système.

Ma santé fut menacée. La terreur venait. Je tombais dans des sommeils de plusieurs jours, et, levé, je continuais les rêves les plus tristes. J'étais mûr pour le trépas, et par une route de dangers ma faiblesse me menait aux confins du monde et de la Cimmérie, patrie de l'ombre et des tourbillons.

Je dus voyager, distraire les enchantements assemblés sur mon cerveau. Sur la mer, que j'aimais comme si elle eût dû me laver d'une souillure, je voyais se lever la croix consolatrice. J'avais été damné par l'arc-en-ciel. Le Bonheur était ma fatalité, mon remords, mon ver: ma vie serait toujours trop immense pour être dévouée à la force et à la beauté.

Le Bonheur! Sa dent, douce à la mort, m'avertissait au chant du coq,—*ad matutinum,* au *Christus venit,*—dans les plus sombres villes:

> Ô saisons, ô châteaux!
> Quelle âme est sans défauts?
>
> J'ai fait la magique étude
> Du bonheur, qu'aucun n'élude.
>
> Salut à lui, chaque fois
> Que chante le coq gaulois.
>
> Ah! je n'aurai plus d'envie:
> Il s'est chargé de ma vie.
>
> Ce charme a pris âme et corps
> Et dispersé les efforts.
>
> Ô saisons, ô châteaux!
> L'heure de sa fuite, hélas!
> Sera l'heure du trépas.
>
> Ô saisons, ô châteaux!

Cela s'est passé. Je sais aujourd'hui saluer la beauté.

L'IMPOSSIBLE

Ah! cette vie de mon enfance, la grande route par tous les temps, sobre sur-naturellement, plus désintéressé que le meilleur des mendiants, fier de n'avoir ni pays, ni amis, quelle sottise c'était.—Et je m'en aperçois seulement!

—J'ai eu raison de mépriser ces bonshommes qui ne perdraient pas l'occasion d'une caresse, parasites de la propreté et de la santé de nos femmes, aujourd'hui qu'elles sont si peu d'accord avec nous.

J'ai eu raison dans tous mes dédains: puisque je m'évade!

Je m'évade!

Je m'explique.

Hier encore, je soupirais: «Ciel! sommes-nous assez de damnés ici-bas! Moi j'ai tant de temps déjà dans leur troupe! Je les connais tous. Nous nous reconnaissons toujours; nous nous dégoûtons. La charité nous est inconnue. Mais nous sommes polis; nos relations avec le monde sont très-convenables.» Est-ce étonnant? Le monde! les marchands, les naïfs!—Nous ne sommes pas déshonorés.—Mais les élus, comment nous recevraient-ils? Or il y a des gens hargneux et joyeux, de faux élus, puisqu'il nous faut de l'audace ou de l'humilité pour les aborder. Ce sont les seuls élus. Ce ne sont pas des bénisseurs!

M'étant retrouvé deux sous de raison—ça passe vite!—je vois que mes malaises viennent de ne m'être pas figuré assez tôt que nous sommes à l'Occident. Les marais occidentaux! Non que je croie la lumière altérée, la forme exténuée, le mouvement égaré … Bon! voici que mon esprit veut absolument se charger de tous les développements cruels qu'a subis l'esprit depuis la fin de l'Orient … Il en veut, mon esprit!

… Mes deux sous de raison sont finis!—L'esprit est autorité, il veut que je sois en Occident Il faudrait le faire taire pour conclure comme je voulais.

J'envoyais au diable les palmes des martyrs, les rayons de l'art, l'orgueil des inventeurs, l'ardeur des pillards; je retournais à l'Orient et à la sagesse première et éternelle.—Il paraît que c'est un rêve de paresse grossière!

Pourtant, je ne songeais guère au plaisir d'échapper aux souffrances modernes. Je n'avais pas en vue la sagesse bâtarde du Coran.—Mais n'y a-t-il pas un supplice réel en ce que, depuis cette déclaration de la science, le christianisme, l'homme *se joue,* se prouve les évidences, se gonfle du plaisir de répéter ces preuves, et ne vit que comme cela! Torture subtile, niaise; source de mes divagations spirituelles. La nature pourrait s'ennuyer, peut-être~! M. Prudhomme est né avec le Christ.

N'est-ce pas parce que nous cultivons la brume! Nous mangeons la fièvre avec nos légumes aqueux. Et l'ivrognerie! et le tabac! et l'ignorance! et les dévouements!—Tout cela est-il assez loin de la pensée de la sagesse de l'Orient, la patrie primitive? Pourquoi un monde moderne, si de pareils poisons s'inventent!

Les gens d'Église diront: C'est compris. Mais vous voulez parler de l'Éden. Rien pour vous dans l'histoire des peuples orientaux.—C'est vrai; c'est à l'Éden que je songeais! Qu'est-ce que c'est pour mon rêve, cette pureté des races antiques!

Les philosophes: Le monde n'a pas d'âge. L'humanité se déplace, simplement. Vous êtes en Occident, mais libre d'habiter dans votre Orient, quelque ancien qu'il vous le faille,—et d'y habiter bien. Ne soyez pas un vaincu. Philosophes, vous êtes de votre Occident.

Mon esprit, prends garde. Pas de partis de salut violents. Exerce-toi!— Ah! la science ne va pas assez vite pour nous!

—Mais je m'aperçois que mon esprit dort.

S'il était bien éveillé toujours à partir de ce moment, nous serions bientôt à la vérité, qui peut-être nous entoure avec ses anges pleurant!...— S'il avait été éveillé jusqu'à ce moment-ci, c'est que je n'aurais pas cédé aux instincts délétères, à une époque immémoriale!...—S'il avait toujours été bien éveillé, je voguerais en pleine sagesse!...

Ô pureté! pureté!

C'est cette minute d'éveil qui m'a donné la vision de la pureté!—Par l'esprit on va à Dieu!

Déchirante infortune!

L'ÉCLAIR

Le travail humain! c'est l'explosion qui éclaire mon abîme de temps en temps.

«Rien n'est vanité; à la science, et en avant!» crie l'Ecclésiaste moderne, c'est-à-dire *Tout le monde.* Et pourtant les cadavres des méchants et des fainéants tombent sur le cœur des autres...Ah! vite, vite un peu; là-bas, par delà la nuit, ces récompenses futures, éternelles...les échappons-nous?...

—Qu'y puis-je? Je connais le travail; et la science est trop lente. Que la prière galope et que la lumière gronde...je le vois bien. C'est trop simple, et il fait trop chaud; on se passera de moi. J'ai mon devoir, j'en serai fier à la façon de plusieurs, en le mettant de côté.

Ma vie est usée. Allons! feignons, fainéantons, ô pitié! Et nous existerons en nous amusant, en rêvant amours monstres et univers fantastiques, en nous plaignant et en querellant les apparences du monde, saltimbanque, mendiant, artiste, bandit,—prêtre! Sur mon lit d'hôpital, l'odeur de l'encens m'est revenue si puissante; gardien des aromates sacrés, confesseur, martyr...

Je reconnais là ma sale éducation d'enfance. Puis quoi!...Aller mes vingt ans, si les autres vont vingt ans...

Non! non! à présent je me révolte contre la mort! Le travail paraît trop léger à mon orgueil: ma trahison au monde serait un supplice trop court. Au dernier moment, j'attaquerais à droite, à gauche...

Alors,—oh!—chère pauvre âme, l'éternité serait-elle pas perdue pour nous!

MATIN

N'eus-je pas *une fois* une jeunesse aimable, héroïque, fabuleuse, à écrire sur des feuilles d'or,—trop de chance! Par quel crime, par quelle erreur, ai-je mérité ma faiblesse actuelle? Vous qui prétendez que des bêtes poussent des sanglots de chagrin, que des malades désespèrent, que des morts rêvent mal, tâchez de raconter ma chute et mon sommeil. Moi, je ne puis pas plus m'expliquer que le mendiant avec ses continuels *Pater* et *Ave Maria. Je ne sais plus parler!*

Pourtant, aujourd'hui, je crois avoir fini la relation de mon enfer. C'était bien l'enfer; l'ancien, celui dont le fils de l'homme ouvrit les portes.

Du même désert, à la même nuit, toujours mes yeux las se réveillent à l'étoile d'argent, toujours, sans que s'émeuvent les Rois de la vie, les trois mages, le cœur, l'âme, l'esprit. Quand irons-nous, par delà les grèves et les monts, saluer la naissance du travail nouveau, la sagesse nouvelle, la fuite des tyrans et des démons, la fin de la superstition, adorer—les premiers!—Noël sur la terre!

Le chant des cieux, la marche des peuples! Esclaves, ne maudissons pas la vie.

ADIEU

L'automne déjà!—Mais pourquoi regretter un éternel soleil, si nous sommes engagés à la découverte de la clarté divine,—loin des gens qui meurent sur les saisons.

L'automne. Notre barque élevée dans les brumes immobiles tourne vers le port de la misère, la cité énorme au ciel taché de feu et de boue. Ah! les haillons pourris, le pain trempé de pluie, l'ivresse, les mille amours qui m'ont crucifié! Elle ne finira donc point cette goule reine de millions d'âmes et de corps morts *et qui seront jugés!* Je me revois la peau rongée par la boue et la peste, des vers plein les cheveux et les aisselles et encore de plus gros vers dans le cœur, étendu parmi les inconnus sans âge, sans sentiment…J'aurais pu y mourir…L'affreuse évocation! J'exècre la misère.

Et je redoute l'hiver parce que c'est la saison du comfort!

—Quelquefois je vois au ciel des plages sans fin couvertes de blanches nations en joie. Un grand vaisseau d'or, au-dessus de moi, agite ses pavillons multicolores sous les brises du matin. J'ai créé toutes les fêtes, tous les triomphes, tous les drames. J'ai essayé d'inventer de nouvelles fleurs, de nouveaux astres, de nouvelles chairs, de nouvelles langues. J'ai cru acquérir des pouvoirs surnaturels. Eh bien! je dois enterrer mon imagination et mes souvenirs! Une belle gloire d'artiste et de conteur emportée!

Moi! moi qui me suis dit mage ou ange, dispensé de toute morale, je suis rendu au sol, avec un devoir à chercher, et la réalité rugueuse à étreindre! Paysan!

Suis-je trompé? la charité serait-elle sœur de la mort, pour moi?

Enfin, je demanderai pardon pour m'être nourri de mensonge. Et allons.

Mais pas une main amie! et où puiser le secours?

———

Oui, l'heure nouvelle est au moins très sévère.

Car je puis dire que la victoire m'est acquise: les grincements de dents, les sifflements de feu, les soupirs empestés se modèrent. Tous les souvenirs immondes s'effacent. Mes derniers regrets détalent,—des jalousies pour les mendiants, les brigands, les amis de la mort, les arriérés de toutes sortes.—Damnés, si je me vengeais!

Il faut être absolument moderne.

Point de cantiques: tenir le pas gagné. Dure nuit! le sang séché fume sur ma face, et je n'ai rien derrière moi, que cet horrible arbrisseau!... Le combat spirituel est aussi brutal que la bataille d'hommes; mais la vision de la justice est le plaisir de Dieu seul.

Cependant c'est la veille. Recevons tous les influx de vigueur et de tendresse réelle. Et à l'aurore, armés d'une ardente patience, nous entrerons aux splendides villes.

Que parlais-je de main amie! Un bel avantage, c'est que je puis rire des vieilles amours mensongères, et frapper de honte ces couples menteurs,—j'ai vu l'enfer des femmes là-bas;—et il me sera loisible de *posséder la vérité dans une âme et un corps.*

Avril-août, 1873

Arthur Rimbaud

LES

ILLUMINATIONS

Notice par Paul Verlaine

PARIS

PUBLICATIONS DE *LA VOGUE*

1886

APRÈS LE DÉLUGE

Aussitôt que l'idée du Déluge se fut rassise,

Un lièvre s'arrêta dans les sainfoins et les clochettes mouvantes et dit sa prière à l'arc-en-ciel à travers la toile de l'araignée.

Oh les pierres précieuses qui se cachaient,—les fleurs qui regardaient déjà.

Dans la grande rue sale les étals se dressèrent, et l'on tira les barques vers la mer étagée là-haut comme sur les gravures.

Le sang coula, chez Barbe-Bleue,—aux abattoirs,—dans les cirques, où le sceau de Dieu blêmit les fenêtres. Le sang et le lait coulèrent.

Les castors bâtirent. Les «mazagrans» fumèrent dans les estaminets.

Dans la grande maison de vitres encore ruisselante les enfants en deuil regardèrent les merveilleuses images.

Une porte claqua, et sur la place du hameau, l'enfant tourna ses bras compris des girouettes et des coqs des clochers de partout, sous l'éclatante giboulée.

Madame ★★★ établit un piano dans les Alpes. La messe et les premières communions se célébrèrent aux cent mille autels de la cathédrale.

Les caravanes partirent. Et le Splendide Hôtel fut bâti dans le chaos de glaces et de nuit du pôle.

Depuis lors, la Lune entendit les chacals piaulant par les déserts de thym,—et les églogues en sabots grognant dans le verger. Puis, dans la futaie violette, bourgeonnante, Eucharis me dit que c'était le printemps.

Sourds, étang,—Écume, roule sur le pont et par-dessus les bois;—draps noirs et orgues,—éclairs et tonnerres,—montez et roulez;—Eaux et tristesses, montez et relevez les Déluges.

Car depuis qu'ils se sont dissipés,—oh les pierres précieuses s'enfouissant, et les fleurs ouvertes!—c'est un ennui! et la Reine, la Sorcière qui allume sa braise dans le pot de terre, ne voudra jamais nous raconter ce qu'elle sait, et que nous ignorons.

ENFANCE

I

Cette idole, yeux noirs et crin jaune, sans parents ni cour, plus noble que la fable, mexicaine et flamande; son domaine, azur et verdure insolents, court sur des plages nommées, par des vagues sans vaisseaux, de noms férocement grecs, slaves, celtiques.

À la lisière de la forêt—les fleurs de rêve tintent, éclatent, éclairent,—la fille à lèvre d'orange, les genoux croisés dans le clair déluge qui sourd des prés, nudité qu'ombrent, traversent et habillent les arcs-en-ciel, la flore, la mer.

Dames qui tournoient sur les terrasses voisines de la mer; enfantes et géantes, superbes noires dans la mousse vert-de-gris, bijoux debout sur le sol gras des bosquets et des jardinets dégelés—jeunes mères et grandes sœurs aux regards pleins de pèlerinages, sultanes, princesses de démarche et de costume tyranniques[,] petites étrangères et personnes doucement malheureuses.

Quel ennui, l'heure du «cher corps» et «cher cœur».

II

C'est elle, la petite morte, derrière les rosiers.—La jeune maman trépassée descend le perron—La calèche du cousin crie sur le sable—Le petit frère—(il est aux Indes!) là, devant le couchant, sur le pré d'œillets.—Les vieux qu'on a enterrés tout droits dans le rempart aux giroflées.

L'essaim des feuilles d'or entoure la maison du général. Ils sont dans le midi.—On suit la route rouge pour arriver à l'auberge vide. Le château est à vendre; les persiennes sont détachées.—Le curé aura emporté la clef de l'église.—Autour du parc, les loges des gardes sont inhabitées… Les palissades sont si hautes qu'on ne voit que les cimes bruissantes. D'ailleurs il n'y a rien à voir là dedans.

Les prés remontent aux hameaux sans coqs, sans enclumes. L'écluse est levée. Ô les calvaires et les moulins du désert, les îles et les meules.

Des fleurs magiques bourdonnaient. Les talus *le* berçaient. Des bêtes d'une élégance fabuleuse circulaient. Les nuées s'amassaient sur la haute mer faite d'une éternité de chaudes larmes.

III

Au bois il y a un oiseau, son chant vous arrête et vous fait rougir.

Il y a une horloge qui ne sonne pas.

Il y a une fondrière avec un nid de bêtes blanches.

Il y a une cathédrale qui descend et un lac qui monte.

Il y a une petite voiture abandonnée dans le taillis, ou qui descend le sentier en courant, enrubannée.

Il y a une troupe de petits comédiens en costumes, aperçus sur la route à travers la lisière du bois.

Il y a enfin, quand l'on a faim et soif, quelqu'un qui vous chasse.

IV

Je suis le saint, en prière sur la terrasse,—comme les bêtes pacifiques paissent jusqu'à la mer de Palestine.

Je suis le savant au fauteuil sombre. Les branches et la pluie se jettent à la croisée de la bibliothèque.

Je suis le piéton de la grand'route par les bois nains; la rumeur des écluses couvre mes pas. Je vois longtemps la mélancolique lessive d'or du couchant.

Je serais bien l'enfant abandonné sur la jetée partie à la haute mer, le petit valet, suivant l'allée dont le front touche le ciel.

Les sentiers sont âpres. Les monticules se couvrent de genêts. L'air est immobile. Que les oiseaux et les sources sont loin! Ce ne peut être que la fin du monde, en avançant.

V

Qu'on me loue enfin ce tombeau, blanchi à la chaux avec les lignes du ciment en relief—très loin sous terre.

Je m'accoude à la table, la lampe éclaire très vivement ces journaux que je suis idiot de relire, ces livres sans intérêt.—

À une distance énorme au dessus de mon salon souterrain, les maisons s'implantent, les brumes s'assemblent. La boue est rouge ou noire. Ville monstrueuse, nuit sans fin!

Moins haut, sont des égouts. Aux côtés, rien que l'épaisseur du globe. Peut-être les gouffres d'azur, des puits de feu. C'est peut-être sur ces plans que se rencontrent lunes et comètes, mers et fables.

Aux heures d'amertume je m'imagine des boules de saphir, de métal. Je suis maître du silence. Pourquoi une apparence de soupirail blêmirait-elle au coin de la voûte?

CONTE

Un Prince était vexé de ne s'être employé jamais qu'à la perfection des générosités vulgaires. Il prévoyait d'étonnantes révolutions de l'amour, et soupçonnait ses femmes de pouvoir mieux que cette complaisance agrémentée de ciel et de luxe. Il voulait voir la vérité, l'heure du désir et de la satisfaction essentiels. Que ce fût ou non une aberration de piété, il voulut. Il possédait au moins un assez large pouvoir humain.

—Toutes les femmes qui l'avaient connu furent assassinées. Quel saccage du jardin de la beauté! Sous le sabre, elles le bénirent. Il n'en commanda point de nouvelles.—Les femmes réapparurent.

Il tua tous ceux qui le suivaient, après la chasse ou les libations.—Tous le suivaient.

Il s'amusa à égorger les bêtes de luxe. Il fit flamber les palais. Il se ruait sur les gens et les taillait en pièces.—La foule, les toits d'or, les belles bêtes existaient encore.

Peut-on s'extasier dans la destruction, se rajeunir par la cruauté! Le peuple ne murmura pas. Personne n'offrit le concours de ses vues.

Un soir il galopait fièrement. Un Génie apparut, d'une beauté ineffable, inavouable même. De sa physionomie et de son maintien ressortait la promesse d'un amour multiple et complexe! d'un bonheur indicible, insupportable même! Le Prince et le Génie s'anéantirent probablement dans la santé essentielle. Comment n'auraient-ils pas pu en mourir? Ensemble donc ils moururent.

Mais ce Prince décéda, dans son palais, à un âge ordinaire. Le prince était le Génie. Le Génie était le Prince.

La musique savante manque à notre désir.

PARADE

Des drôles très solides. Plusieurs ont exploité vos mondes. Sans besoins, et peu pressés de mettre en œuvre leurs brillantes facultés et leur expérience de vos consciences. Quels hommes mûrs! Des yeux hébétés à la façon de la nuit d'été, rouges et noirs, tricolores, d'acier piqué d'étoiles d'or; des faciès déformés, plombés, blêmis[,] incendiés; des enrouements folâtres! La démarche cruelle des oripeaux!—Il y a quelques jeunes,—comment regarderaient-ils Chérubin?—pourvus de voix effrayantes et de quelques ressources dangereuses. On les envoie prendre du dos en ville, affublés d'un *luxe* dégoûtant.

Ô le plus violent Paradis de la grimace enragée! Pas de comparaison avec vos Fakirs et les autres bouffonneries scéniques. Dans des costumes improvisés avec le goût du mauvais rêve ils jouent des complaintes, des tragédies de malandrins et de demi-dieux spirituels comme l'histoire ou les religions ne l'ont jamais été, Chinois, Hottentots, bohémiens, niais, hyènes, Molochs, vieilles démences, démons sinistres, ils mêlent les tours populaires, maternels, avec les poses et les tendresses bestiales. Ils interpréteraient des pièces nouvelles et des chansons «bonnes filles». Maîtres jongleurs, ils transforment le lieu et les personnes et usent de la comédie magnétique. Les yeux flambent, le sang chante, les os s'élargissent, les larmes et des filets rouges ruissellent. Leur raillerie ou leur terreur dure une minute, ou des mois entiers.

J'ai seul la clef de cette parade sauvage.

ANTIQUE

Gracieux fils de Pan! Autour de ton front couronné de fleurettes et de baies tes yeux, des boules précieuses, remuent. Tachées de lies brunes, tes joues se creusent. Tes crocs luisent. Ta poitrine ressemble à une cithare, des tintements circulent dans tes bras blonds. Ton cœur bat dans ce ventre où dort le double sexe. Promène-toi, la nuit, en mouvant doucement cette cuisse, cette seconde cuisse et cette jambe de gauche.

BEING BEAUTEOUS

Devant une neige un Être de Beauté de haute taille. Des sifflements de mort et des cercles de musique sourde font monter, s'élargir et trembler comme un spectre ce corps adoré; des blessures écarlates et noires éclatent dans les chairs superbes. Les couleurs propres de la vie se foncent, dansent, et se dégagent autour de la Vision, sur le chantier. Et les frissons s'élèvent et grondent et la saveur forcenée de ces effets se chargeant avec les sifflements mortels et les rauques musiques que le monde, loin derrière nous, lance sur notre mère de beauté,—elle recule, elle se dresse. Oh! nos os sont revêtus d'un nouveau corps amoureux.

★   ★   ★   ★

Ô la face cendrée, l'écusson de crin, les bras de cristal! le canon sur lequel je dois m'abattre à travers la mêlée des arbres et de l'air léger!

VIES

I

Ô les énormes avenues du pays saint, les terrasses du temple! Qu'a-t-on fait du brahmane qui m'expliqua les Proverbes? D'alors, de là-bas, je vois encore même les vieilles! Je me souviens des heures d'argent et de soleil vers les fleuves, la main de la campagne sur mon épaule, et de nos caresses debout dans les plaines poivrées.—Un envol de pigeons écarlates tonne autour de ma pensée.—Exilé ici j'ai eu une scène où jouer les chefs-d'œuvre dramatiques de toutes les littératures. Je vous indiquerais les richesses inouïes. J'observe l'histoire des trésors que vous trouvâtes. Je vois la suite! Ma sagesse est aussi dédaignée que le chaos. Qu'est mon néant, auprès de la stupeur qui vous attend?

II

Je suis un inventeur bien autrement méritant que tous ceux qui m'ont précédé; un musicien même, qui ai trouvé quelque chose comme la clef de l'amour. À présent, gentilhomme d'une campagne aigre au ciel sobre j'essaie de m'émouvoir au souvenir de l'enfance mendiante, de l'apprentissage ou de l'arrivée en sabots, des polémiques, des cinq ou six veuvages, et quelques noces où ma forte tête m'empêcha de monter au diapason des camarades. Je ne regrette pas ma vieille part de gaîté divine: l'air sobre de cette aigre campagne alimente fort activement mon atroce scepticisme. Mais comme ce scepticisme ne peut désormais être mis en œuvre, et que d'ailleurs je suis dévoué à un trouble nouveau,—j'attends de devenir un très méchant fou.

III

Dans un grenier où je fus enfermé à douze ans j'ai connu le monde, j'ai illustré la comédie humaine. Dans un cellier j'ai appris l'histoire. À quelque fête de nuit dans une cité du Nord j'ai rencontré toutes les femmes des anciens peintres. Dans un vieux passage à Paris on m'a enseigné les sciences classiques. Dans une magnifique demeure cernée par l'Orient entier j'ai accompli mon immense œuvre et passé mon illustre retraite. J'ai brassé mon sang. Mon devoir m'est remis. Il ne faut même plus songer à cela. Je suis réellement d'outre-tombe, et pas de commissions.

DÉPART

Assez vu. La vision s'est rencontrée à tous les airs.

Assez eu. Rumeurs des villes, le soir, et au soleil, et toujours.

Assez connu. Les arrêts de la vie.—Ô Rumeurs et Visions!

Départ dans l'affection et le bruit neufs!

ROYAUTÉ

Un beau matin, chez un peuple fort doux, un homme et une femme superbes criaient sur la place publique. «Mes amis, je veux qu'elle soit reine!» «Je veux être reine!» Elle riait et tremblait. Il parlait aux amis de révélation, d'épreuve terminée. Ils se pâmaient l'un contre l'autre.

En effet ils furent rois toute une matinée où les tentures carminées se relevèrent sur les maisons, et toute l'après-midi, où ils s'avancèrent du côté des jardins de palmes.

À UNE RAISON

Un coup de ton doigt sur le tambour décharge tous les sons et commence la nouvelle harmonie.

Un pas de toi, c'est la levée des nouveaux hommes et leur en-marche.

Ta tête se détourne: le nouvel amour! Ta tête se retourne,—le nouvel amour!

«Change nos lots, crible les fléaux, à commencer par le temps», te chantent ces enfants. «Élève n'importe où la substance de nos fortunes et de nos vœux» on t'en prie,

Arrivée de toujours, qui t'en iras partout.

MATINÉE D'IVRESSE

Ô *mon* Bien! Ô *mon* Beau! Fanfare atroce où je ne trébuche point! Chevalet féerique! Hourra pour l'œuvre inouïe et pour le corps merveilleux, pour la première fois! Cela commença sous les rires des enfants, cela finira par eux. Ce poison va rester dans toutes nos veines même quand, la fanfare tournant, nous serons rendu à l'ancienne inharmonie. Ô maintenant nous si digne de ces tortures! rassemblons fervemment cette promesse surhumaine faite à notre corps et à notre âme créés: cette promesse, cette démence! L'élégance, la science, la violence! On nous a promis d'enterrer dans l'ombre l'arbre du bien et du mal, de déporter les honnêtetés tyranniques, afin que nous amenions notre très pur amour. Cela commença par quelques dégoûts et cela finit,—ne pouvant nous saisir sur[-]le[-]champ de cette éternité,—cela finit par une débandade de parfums.

Rire des enfants, discrétion des esclaves, austérité des vierges, horreur des figures et des objets d'ici, sacrés soyez-vous par le souvenir de cette veille. Cela commençait par toute la rustrerie, voici que cela finit par des anges de flamme et de glace.

Petite veille d'ivresse, sainte! quand ce ne serait que pour le masque dont tu nous a[s] gratifié. Nous t'affirmons, méthode! Nous n'oublions pas que tu as glorifié hier chacun de nos âges. Nous avons foi au poison. Nous savons donner notre vie tout entière tous les jours.

Voici le temps des *Assassins.*

PHRASES

Quand le monde sera réduit en un seul bois noir pour nos quatre yeux étonnés,—en une plage pour deux enfants fidèles—en une maison musicale pour notre claire sympathie,—je vous trouverai.

Qu'il n'y ait ici[-]bas qu'un vieillard seul, calme et beau, entouré d'un «luxe inouï»,—et je suis à vos genoux.

Que j'aie réalisé tous vos souvenirs,—que je sois celle qui sait vous garrotter,—je vous étoufferai.

————

Quand nous sommes très forts,—qui recule? très gais, qui tombe de ridicule? Quand nous sommes très méchants, que ferait-on de nous.

Parez-vous, dansez, riez.—Je ne pourrai jamais envoyer l'Amour par la fenêtre.

————

—Ma camarade, mendiante, enfant monstre! comme ça t'est égal, ces malheureuses et ces manœuvres, et mes embarras. Attache-toi à nous avec ta voix impossible, ta voix! unique flatteur de ce vil désespoir.

FRAGMENTS SANS TITRE

Une matinée couverte, en Juillet. Un goût de cendres vole dans l'air;—une odeur de bois suant dans l'âtre,—les fleurs rouies—le saccage des promenades—la bruine des canaux par les champs,—pourquoi pas déjà les joujoux et l'encens?

———

J'ai tendu des cordes de clocher à clocher; des guirlandes de fenêtre à fenêtre; des chaînes d'or d'étoile à étoile, et je danse.

———

Le haut étang fume continuellement. Quelle sorcière va se dresser sur le couchant blanc? Quelles violettes frondaisons vont descendre?

———

Pendant que les fonds publics s'écoulent en fêtes de fraternité, il sonne une cloche de feu rose dans les nuages.

———

Avivant un agréable goût d'encre de Chine une poudre noire pleut doucement sur ma veillée.—Je baisse les feux du lustre, je me jette sur le lit, et tourné du côté de l'ombre je vous vois, mes filles! mes reines!

OUVRIERS

Ô cette chaude matinée de février. Le Sud inopportun vint relever nos souvenirs d'indigents absurdes, notre jeune misère.

Henrika avait une jupe de coton à carreau blanc et brun, qui a dû être portée au siècle dernier, un bonnet à rubans et un foulard de soie. C'était bien plus triste qu'un deuil. Nous faisions un tour dans la banlieue. Le temps était couvert et ce vent du Sud excitait toutes les vilaines odeurs des jardins ravagés et des prés desséchés.

Cela ne devait pas fatiguer ma femme au même point que moi. Dans une flache laissée par l'inondation du mois précédent à un sentier assez haut elle me fit remarquer de très petits poissons.

La ville, avec sa fumée et ses bruits de métiers, nous suivait très loin dans les chemins. Ô l'autre monde, l'habitation bénie par le ciel et les ombrages! Le sud me rappelait les misérables incidents de mon enfance, mes désespoirs d'été, l'horrible quantité de force et de science que le sort a toujours éloignée de moi. Non! Nous ne passerons pas l'été dans cet avare pays où nous ne serons jamais que des orphelins fiancés. Je veux que ce bras durci ne traîne plus *une chère image.*

LES PONTS

Des ciels gris de cristal. Un bizarre dessin de ponts, ceux-ci droits, ceux-là bombés, d'autres descendant ou obliquant en angles sur les premiers, et ces figures se renouvelant dans les autres circuits éclairés du canal, mais tous tellement longs et légers que les rives, chargées de dômes[,] s'abaissent et s'amoindrissent. Quelques-uns de ces ponts sont encore chargés de masures. D'autres soutiennent des mâts, des signaux, de frêles parapets. Des accords mineurs se croisent, et filent, des cordes montent des berges. On distingue une veste rouge, peut-être d'autres costumes et des instruments de musique. Sont-ce des airs populaires, des bouts de concerts seigneuriaux, des restants d'hymnes publics? L'eau est grise et bleue, large comme un bras de mer.—Un rayon blanc, tombant du haut du ciel, anéantit cette comédie.

VILLE

Je suis un éphémère et point trop mécontent citoyen d'une métropole crue moderne parce que tout goût connu a été éludé dans les ameublements et l'extérieur des maisons aussi bien que dans le plan de la ville. Ici vous ne signaleriez les traces d'aucun monument de superstition. La morale et la langue sont réduites à leur plus simple expression, enfin! Ces millions de gens qui n'ont pas besoin de se connaître amènent si pareillement l'éducation, le métier et la vieillesse, que ce cours de vie doit être plusieurs fois moins long que ce qu'une statistique folle trouve pour les peuples du continent. Aussi comme, de ma fenêtre, je vois des spectres nouveaux roulant à travers l'épaisse et éternelle fumée de charbon,— notre ombre des bois, notre nuit d'été!—des Érynnies nouvelles, devant mon cottage qui est ma patrie et tout mon cœur puisque tout ici ressemble à ceci,—la Mort sans pleurs, notre active fille et servante, et un Amour désespéré, et un joli Crime piaulant dans la boue de la rue.

ORNIÈRES

À droite l'aube d'été éveille les feuilles et les vapeurs et les bruits de ce coin du parc, et les talus de gauche tiennent dans leur ombre violette les mille rapides ornières de la route humide. Défilé de féeries. En effet: des chars chargés d'animaux de bois doré, de mâts et de toiles bariolées, au grand galop de vingt chevaux de cirque tachetés, et les enfants et les hommes sur leurs bêtes les plus étonnantes;—vingt véhicules, bossés, pavoisés et fleuris comme des carrosses anciens ou de contes, pleins d'enfants attifés pour une pastorale suburbaine;—Même des cercueils sous leur dais de nuit dressant les panaches d'ébène, filant au trot des grandes juments bleues et noirs.

VILLES [I]

Ce sont des villes! C'est un peuple pour qui se sont montés ces Alleghanys et ces Libans de rêve! Des chalets de cristal et de bois qui se meuvent sur des rails et des poulies invisibles. Les vieux cratères ceints de colosses et de palmiers de cuivre rugissent mélodieusement dans les feux. Des fêtes amoureuses sonnent sur les canaux pendus derrière les chalets. La chasse des carillons crie dans les gorges. Des corporations de chanteurs géants accourent dans des vêtements et des oriflammes éclatants comme la lumière des cimes. Sur les plate[s-]formes au milieu des gouffres les Rolands sonnent leur bravoure. Sur les passerelles de l'abîme et les toits des auberges l'ardeur du ciel pavoise les mâts. L'écroulement des apothéoses rejoint les champs des hauteurs où les centauresses séraphiques évoluent parmi les avalanches. Au[-]dessus du niveau des plus hautes crêtes une mer troublée par la naissance éternelle de Vénus, chargée de flottes orphéoniques et de la rumeur des perles et des conques précieuses,—la mer s'assombrit parfois avec des éclats mortels. Sur les versants des moissons de fleurs grandes comme nos armes et nos coupes, mugissent. Des cortèges de Mabs en robes rousses, opalines, montent des ravines. Là[-]haut, les pieds dans la cascade et les ronces, les cerfs tettent Diane. Les Bacchantes des banlieues sanglotent et la lune brûle et hurle. Vénus entre dans les cavernes des forgerons et des ermites. Des groupes de beffrois chantent les idées des peuples. Des châteaux bâtis en os sort la musique inconnue. Toutes les légendes évoluent et les élans se ruent dans les bourgs. Le paradis des orages s'effondre. Les sauvages dansent sans cesse la fête de la nuit. Et une heure je suis descendu dans le mouvement d'un boulevard de Bagdad où des compagnies ont chanté la joie du travail nouveau, sous une brise épaisse, circulant sans pouvoir éluder les fabuleux fantômes des monts où l'on a dû se retrouver.

Quels bons bras, quelle belle heure me rendront cette région d'où viennent mes sommeils et mes moindres mouvements?

VAGABONDS

Pitoyable frère! Que d'atroces veillées je lui dus! «Je ne me saisissais pas fervemment de cette entreprise. Je m'étais joué de son infirmité. Par ma faute nous retournerions en exil, en esclavage.» Il me supposait un guignon et une innocence très-bizarres, et il ajoutait des raisons inquiétantes.

Je répondais en ricanant à ce satanique docteur, et finissais par gagner la fenêtre. Je créais, par delà la campagne traversée par des bandes de musique rare, les fantômes du futur luxe nocturne.

Après cette distraction vaguement hygiénique, je m'étendais sur une paillasse. Et, presque chaque nuit, aussitôt endormi, le pauvre frère se levait, la bouche pourrie, les yeux arrachés,—tel qu'il se rêvait!—et me tirait dans la salle en hurlant son songe de chagrin idiot.

J'avais en effet, en toute sincérité d'esprit, pris l'engagement de le rendre à son état primitif de fils du soleil,—et nous errions, nourris du vin des cavernes et du biscuit de la route, moi pressé de trouver le lieu et la formule.

VILLES[II]

L'acropole officielle outre les conceptions de la barbarie moderne les plus colossales. Impossible d'exprimer le jour mat produit par ce ciel immuablement gris, l'éclat impérial des bâtisses, et la neige éternelle du sol. On a reproduit dans un goût d'énormité singulier toutes les merveilles classiques de l'architecture. J'assiste à des expositions de peinture dans des locaux vingt fois plus vastes qu'Hampton-Court. Quelle peinture! Un Nabuchodonosor norwégien a fait construire les escaliers des ministères; les subalternes que j'ai pu voir sont déjà plus fiers que des Brahmas et j'ai tremblé à l'aspect des gardiens de colosses et officiers de constructions. Par le groupement des bâtiments en squares, cours et terrasses fermées, on [a] évincé les cochers. Les parcs représentent la nature primitive travaillée par un art superbe. Le haut quartier a des parties inexplicables: un bras de mer, sans bateaux, roule sa nappe de grésil bleu entre des quais chargés de candélabres géants. Un pont court conduit à une poterne immédiatement sous le dôme de la Sainte-Chapelle. Ce dôme est une armature d'acier artistique de quinze mille pieds de diamètre environ.

Sur quelques points des passerelles de cuivre, des plates-formes, des escaliers qui contournent les halles et les piliers, j'ai cru pouvoir juger la profondeur de la ville. C'est le prodige dont je n'ai pu me rendre compte: quels sont les niveaux des autres quartiers sur ou sous l'acropole? Pour l'étranger de notre temps la reconnaissance est impossible. Le quartier commerçant est un circus d'un seul style, avec galeries à arcades. On ne voit pas de boutiques. Mais la neige de la chaussée est écrasée; quelques nababs aussi rares que les promeneurs d'un matin de dimanche à Londres, se dirigent vers une diligence de diamants. Quelques divans de velours rouge: on sert des boissons polaires dont le prix varie de huit cent[s] à huit mille roupies. À l'idée de chercher des théâtres sur ce circus, je me réponds que les boutiques doivent contenir des drames assez-sombres. Je pense qu'il y a une police; mais la loi doit être tellement étrange, que je renonce à me faire une idée des aventuriers d'ici.

Le faubourg aussi élégant qu'une belle rue de Paris est favorisé d'un air de lumière. L'élément démocratique compte quelques cents âmes. Là encore les maisons ne se suivent pas; le faubourg se perd bizarrement dans la campagne, le «Comté» qui remplit l'occident éternel des forêts et des plantations prodigieuses où les gentilshommes sauvages chassent leurs chroniques sous la lumière qu'on a créée.

VEILLÉES

I

C'est le repos éclairé, ni fièvre ni langueur, sur le lit ou sur le pré.

C'est l'ami ni ardent ni faible. L'ami.

C'est l'aimée ni tourmentante ni tourmentée. L'aimée.

L'air et le monde point cherchés. La vie.

—Était-ce donc ceci?

—Et le rêve fraîchit.

II

L'éclairage revient à l'arbre de bâtisse. Des deux extrémités de la salle, décors quelconques, des élévations harmoniques se joignent. La muraille en face du veilleur est une succession psychologique de coupes de frises, de bandes atmosphériques et d'accidences géologiques.—Rêve intense et rapide de groupes sentimentaux avec des êtres de tous les caractères parmi toutes les apparences.

III

Les lampes et les tapis de la veillée font le bruit des vagues, la nuit, le long de la coque et autour du steerage.

La mer de la veillée, telle que les seins d'Amélie.

Les tapisseries, jusqu'à mi-hauteur, des taillis de dentelle, teinte d'émeraude, où se jettent les tourterelles de la veillée.

. . . .

La plaque du foyer noir, de réels soleils des grèves: ah! puits des magies; seule vue d'aurore, cette fois.

MYSTIQUE

Sur la pente du talus les anges tournent leurs robes de laine dans les herbages d'acier et d'émeraude.

Des prés de flammes bondissent jusqu'au sommet du mamelon. À gauche le terreau de l'arête est piétiné par tous les homicides et toutes les batailles, et tous les bruits désastreux filent leur courbe. Derrière l'arête de droite la ligne des orients, des progrès.

Et tandis que la bande en haut du tableau est formée de la rumeur tournante et bondissante des conques des mers et des nuits humaines,

La douceur fleurie des étoiles et du ciel et du reste descend en face du talus, comme un panier,—contre notre face, et fait l'abîme fleurant et bleu là-dessous.

AUBE

J'ai embrassé l'aube d'été.

Rien ne bougeait encore au front des palais. L'eau était morte. Les camps d'ombres ne quittaient pas la route du bois. J'ai marché, réveillant les haleines vives et tièdes, et les pierreries regardèrent, et les ailes se levèrent sans bruit.

La première entreprise fut, dans le sentier déjà empli de frais et blêmes éclats, une fleur qui me dit son nom.

Je ris au wasserfall blond qui s'échevela à travers les sapins: à la cime argentée je reconnus la déesse.

Alors je levai un à un les voiles. Dans l'allée, en agitant les bras. Par la plaine, où je l'ai dénoncée au coq. À la grand'ville elle fuyait parmi les clochers et les dômes, et courant comme un mendiant sur les quais de marbre, je la chassais.

En haut de la route, près d'un bois de lauriers, je l'ai entourée avec ses voiles amassés, et j'ai senti un peu son immense corps. L'aube et l'enfant tombèrent au bas du bois.

Au réveil il était midi.

FLEURS

D'un gradin d'or,—parmi les cordons de soie, les gazes grises, les velours verts et les disques de cristal qui noircissent comme du bronze au soleil,—je vois la digitale s'ouvrir sur un tapis de filigranes d'argent, d'yeux et de chevelures.

Des pièces d'or jaune semées sur l'agate, des piliers d'acajou supportant un dôme d'émeraudes, des bouquets de satin blanc et de fines verges de rubis entourent la rose d'eau.

Tels qu'un dieu aux énormes yeux bleus et aux formes de neige, la mer et le ciel attirent aux terrasses de marbre la foule des jeunes et fortes roses.

NOCTURNE VULGAIRE

Un souffle ouvre des brèches opéradiques dans les cloisons,—brouille le pivotement des toits rongés,—disperse les limites de foyers,—éclipse les croisées.—Le long de la vigne, m'étant appuyé du pied à une gargouille,—je suis descendu dans ce carrosse dont l'époque est assez indiquée par les glaces convexes, les panneaux bombés et les sophas contournés— Corbillard de mon sommeil, isolé, maison de berger de ma niaiserie, le véhicule vire sur le gazon de la grande route effacée: et dans un défaut en haut de la glace de droite tournoient les blêmes figures lunaires, feuilles, seins;—Un vert et un bleu très foncés envahissent l'image. Dételage aux environs d'une tache de gravier.

—Ici va-t-on siffler pour l'orage, et les Sodomes,—et les Solymes,—et les bêtes féroces et les armées,

(—Postillon et bêtes de Songe reprendront-ils sous les plus suffocantes futaies, pour m'enfoncer jusqu'aux yeux dans la source de soie.)

—Et nous envoyer, fouettés à travers les eaux clapotantes et les boissons répandues, rouler sur l'aboi des dogues…

—Un souffle disperse les limites du foyer.

MARINE

Les chars d'argent et de cuivre—
Les proues d'acier et d'argent—
Battent l'écume,—
Soulèvent les souches des ronces—
        Les courants de la lande,
Et les ornières immenses du reflux
Filent circulairement vers l'est,
Vers les piliers de la forêt,—
Vers les fûts de la jetée,
Dont l'angle est heurté
   par des tourbillons de lumière

FÊTE D'HIVER

La cascade sonne derrière les huttes d'opéra-comique. Des girandoles prolongent, dans les vergers et les allées voisins du Méandre,—les verts et les rouges du couchant. Nymphes d'Horace coiffées au Premier Empire,—Rondes Sibériennes, Chinoises de Boucher.

ANGOISSE

Se peut-il qu'Elle me fasse pardonner les ambitions continuellement écrasées,—qu'une fin aisée répare les âges d'indigence,—qu'un jour de succès nous endorme sur la honte de notre inhabileté fatale,

(Ô palmes! diamant!—Amour, force!—plus haut que toutes joies et gloires!—de toutes façons, partout,—démon, dieu,—Jeunesse de cet être-ci; moi!)

Que des accidents de féerie scientifique et des mouvements de fraternité sociale soient chéris comme restitution progressive de la franchise première?...

Mais la Vampire qui nous rend gentils commande que nous nous amusions avec ce qu'elle nous laisse, ou qu'autrement nous soyons plus drôles.

Rouler aux blessures, par l'air lassant et la mer; aux supplices, par le silence des eaux et de l'air meurtriers; aux tortures qui rient, dans leur silence atrocement houleux.

MÉTROPOLITAIN

Du détroit d'indigo aux mers d'Ossian, sur le sable rose et orange qu'a lavé le ciel vineux viennent de monter et de se croiser des boulevards de cristal habités incontinent par des jeunes familles pauvres qui s'alimentent chez les fruitiers. Rien de riche.—La ville!

Du désert de bitume fuient droit en déroute avec les nappes de brumes échelonnées en bandes affreuses au ciel qui se recourbe, se recule et descend, formé de la plus sinistre fumée noire que puisse faire l'Océan en deuil, les casques, les roues, les barques, les croupes.—La bataille!

Lève la tête: ce pont de bois, arqué; les derniers potagers de Samarie; ces masques enluminés sous la lanterne fouettée par la nuit froide; l'ondine niaise à la robe bruyante, au bas de la rivière; les crânes lumineux dans les plants de pois,—et les autres fantasmagories—la campagne.

Des routes bordées de grilles et de murs, contenant à peine leurs bosquets, et les atroces fleurs qu'on appellerait cœurs et sœurs, Damas damnant de longueur,—possessions de féeriques aristocraties ultra-Rhénanes, Japonaises, Guaranies, propres encore à recevoir la musique des anciens—et il y a des auberges qui pour toujours n'ouvrent déjà plus—il y a des princesses, et si tu n'es pas trop accablé, l'étude des astres—le ciel.

Le matin où avec Elle vous vous débattîtes parmi les éclats de neige, les lèvres vertes, les glaces, les drapeaux noirs et les rayons bleus, et les parfums pourpres du soleil des pôles,—ta force.

BARBARE

Bien après les jours et les saisons, et les êtres et les pays,

Le pavillon en viande saignante sur la soie des mers et des fleurs arctiques; (elles n'existent pas.)

Remis des vieilles fanfares d'héroïsme—qui nous attaquent encore le cœur et la tête—loin des anciens assassins—

Oh! le pavillon en viande saignante sur la soie des mers et des fleurs arctiques; (elles n'existent pas)

Douceurs!

Les brasiers, pleuvant aux rafales de givre,—Douceurs!—les feux à la pluie du vent de diamants—jetée par le cœur terrestre éternellement carbonisé pour nous.—Ô monde!—

(Loin des vieilles retraites et des vieilles flammes, qu'on entend, qu'on sent,)

Les brasiers et les écumes. La musique, virement des gouffres et choc des glaçons aux astres.

Ô Douceurs, ô monde, ô musique! Et là, les formes, les sueurs, les chevelures et les yeux, flottant. Et les larmes blanches, bouillantes,— ô douceurs!—et la voix féminine arrivée au fond des volcans et des grottes arctiques.

Le pavillon...

FAIRY

Pour Hélène se conjurèrent les sèves ornementales dans les ombres vierges et les clartés impassibles dans le silence astral. L'ardeur de l'été fut confiée à des oiseaux muets et l'indolence requise à une barque de deuils sans prix par des anses d'amours morts et de parfums affaissés.

—Après le moment de l'air des bûcheronnes à la rumeur du torrent sous la ruine des bois, de la sonnerie des bestiaux à l'écho des vals, et des cris des steppes.—

Pour l'enfance d'Hélène frissonnèrent les fourrures et les ombres,—et le sein des pauvres, et les légendes du ciel.

Et ses yeux et sa danse supérieurs encore aux éclats précieux, aux influences froides, au plaisir du décor et de l'heure uniques.

GUERRE

Enfant, certains ciels ont affiné mon optique: tous les caractères nuancèrent ma physionomie. Les Phénomènes s'émurent.—À présent, l'inflexion éternelle des moments et l'infini des mathématiques me chassent par ce monde où je subis tous les succès civils, respecté de l'enfance étrange et des affections énormes.—Je songe à une Guerre, de droit ou de force, de logique bien imprévue.

C'est aussi simple qu'une phrase musicale.

SOLDE

À vendre ce que les Juifs n'ont pas vendu, ce que noblesse ni crime n'ont goûté, ce qu'ignore l'amour maudit et la probité infernale des masses: ce que le temps ni la science n'ont pas à reconnaître;

Les Voix reconstituées; l'éveil fraternel de toutes les énergies chorales et orchestrales et leurs applications instantanées; l'occasion, unique, de dégager nos sens!

À vendre les Corps sans prix, hors de toute race, de tout monde, de tout sexe, de toute descendance! Les richesses jaillissant à chaque démarche! Solde de diamants sans contrôle!

À vendre l'anarchie pour les masses; la satisfaction irrépressible pour les amateurs supérieurs; la mort atroce pour les fidèles et les amants!

À vendre les habitations et les migrations, sports, féeries et comforts parfaits, et le bruit, le mouvement et l'avenir qu'ils font!

À vendre les applications de calcul et les sauts d'harmonie inouïs. Les trouvailles et les termes non soupçonnés, possession immédiate.

Élan insensé et infini aux splendeurs invisibles, aux délices insensibles,—et ses secrets affolants pour chaque vice—et sa gaîté effrayante pour la foule—

À vendre les Corps, les voix, l'immense opulence inquestionable, ce qu'on ne vendra jamais. Les vendeurs ne sont pas à bout de solde! Les voyageurs n'ont pas à rendre leur commission de si tôt!

JEUNESSE

I
Dimanche

Les calculs de côté, l'inévitable descente du ciel, et la visite des souvenirs et la séance des rhythmes occupent la demeure, la tête et le monde de l'esprit.

—Un cheval détale sur le turf suburbain et le long des cultures et des boisements percé par la peste carbonique. Une misérable femme de drame, quelque part dans le monde, soupire après des abandons improbables. Les desperadoes languissent après l'orage, l'ivresse et les blessures. De petits enfants étouffent des malédictions le long des rivières.—

Reprenons l'étude au bruit de l'œuvre dévorante qui se rassemble et remonte dans les masses.

II
Sonnet

Homme de constitution ordinaire, la chair
n'était-elle pas un fruit pendu dans le verger,—ô
journées enfantes! le corps un trésor à prodiguer;—ô
aimer, le péril ou la force de Psyché? La terre
avait des versants fertiles en princes et en artistes,
et la descendance et la race vous poussaient aux
crimes et aux deuils: le monde votre fortune et votre
péril. Mais à présent, ce labeur comblé, toi, tes calculs,
—toi, tes impatiences—ne sont plus que votre danse et
votre voix, non fixées et point forcées, quoique d'un double
événement d'invention et de succès une saison,

—en l'humanité fraternelle et discrète par l'univers
sans images;—la force et le droit réfléchissent la danse
et la voix à présent seulement appréciées.

III

Vingt ans

Les voix instructives exilées… L'ingénuité physique amèrement rassise…
—Adagio—Ah! l'égoïsme infini de l'adolescence, l'optimisme studieux:
que le monde était plein de fleurs cet été! Les airs et les formes
mourant… Un chœur, pour calmer l'impuissance et l'absence! Un chœur
de verres de mélodies nocturnes… En effet les nerfs vont vite chasser.

IV

Tu en es encore à la tentation d'Antoine. L'ébat du zèle écourté, les
tics d'orgueil puéril, l'affaissement et l'effroi.

Mais tu te mettras à ce travail: toutes les possibilités harmoniques et
architecturales s'émouvront autour de ton siège. Des êtres parfaits, im-
prévus, s'offriront à tes expériences. Dans tes environs affluera rêveuse-
ment la curiosité d'anciennes foules et de luxes oisifs. Ta mémoire et tes
sens ne seront que la nourriture de ton impulsion créatrice. Quant au
monde, quand tu sortiras, que sera-t-il devenu? En tout cas, rien des ap-
parences actuelles.

PROMONTOIRE

L'aube d'or et la soirée frissonnante trouvent notre brick en large en face de cette Villa et de ses dépendances, qui forment un promontoire aussi étendu que l'Épire et le Péloponnèse, ou que la grande île du Japon, ou que l'Arabie! Des fanums qu'éclaire la rentrée des théories, d'immenses vues de la défense des côtes modernes; des dunes illustrées de chaudes fleurs et de bacchanales; de grands canaux de Carthage et des Embankments d'une Venise louche, de molles éruptions d'Etnas et des crevasses de fleurs et d'eaux des glaciers, des lavoirs entourés de peupliers d'Allemagne; des talus de parcs singuliers penchant des têtes d'Arbre du Japon, et les façades circulaires des «Royal» ou des «Grand» de Scarbro' ou de Brooklyn; et leurs railways flanquent, creusent, surplombent les dispositions dans cet Hôtel, choisies dans l'histoire des plus élégantes et des plus colossales constructions de l'Italie, de l'Amérique et de l'Asie, dont les fenêtres et les terrasses à présent pleines d'éclairages, de boissons et de brises riches, sont ouvertes à l'esprit des voyageurs et des nobles—qui permettent, aux heures du jour, à toutes les tarentelles des côtes,—et même aux ritournelles des vallées illustres de l'art, de décorer merveilleusement les façades du Palais-Promontoire.

DÉVOTION

À ma sœur Louise Vanaen de Voringhem:—Sa cornette bleue tournée à la mer du Nord.—Pour les naufragés.

À ma sœur Léonie Aubois d'Ashby. Baou—l'herbe d'été bourdonnante et puante.—Pour la fièvre des mères et des enfants.

À Lulu,—démon—qui a conservé un goût pour les oratoires du temps des Amies et de son éducation incomplète. Pour les hommes! À madame ★★★.

À l'adolescent que je fus. À ce saint vieillard, ermitage ou mission.

À l'esprit des pauvres. Et à un très haut clergé.

Aussi bien à tout culte en telle place de culte mémoriale et parmi tels événements qu'il faille se rendre, suivant les aspirations du moment ou bien notre propre vice sérieux.

Ce soir, à Circeto des hautes glaces, grasse comme le poisson, et enluminée comme les dix mois de la nuit rouge—(son cœur ambre et spunk),—pour ma seule prière muette comme ces régions de nuit et précédant des bravoures plus violentes que ce chaos polaire.

À tout prix et avec tous les airs, même dans des voyages métaphysiques.—Mais plus *alors*.

DÉMOCRATIE

«Le drapeau va au paysage immonde, et notre patois étouffe le tambour.

«Aux centres nous alimenterons la plus cynique prostitution. Nous massacrerons les révoltes logiques.

«Aux pays poivrés et détrempés!—au service des plus monstrueuses exploitations industrielles ou militaires.

«Au revoir ici, n'importe où, Conscrits du bon vouloir, nous aurons la philosophie féroce; ignorants pour la science, roués pour le confort; la crevaison pour le monde qui va. C'est la vraie marche. En avant, route!»

SCÈNES

L'ancienne Comédie poursuit ses accords et divise ses Idylles:
Des boulevards de tréteaux.

Un long pier en bois d'un bout à l'autre d'un champ rocailleux où la foule barbare évolue sous les arbres dépouillés.

Dans des corridors de gaze noire suivant le pas des promeneurs aux lanternes et aux feuilles.

Des oiseaux des mystères s'abattent sur un ponton de maçonnerie mû par l'archipel couvert des embarcations des spectateurs.

Des scènes lyriques accompagnées de flûte et de tambour s'inclinent dans des réduits ménagés sous les plafonds, autour des salons de clubs modernes ou des salles de l'Orient ancien.

La féerie manœuvre au sommet d'un amphithéâtre couronné par les taillis—Ou s'agite et module pour les Béotiens, dans l'ombre des futaies mouvantes sur l'arête des cultures.

L'opéra-comique se divise sur une scène à l'arête d'intersection de dix cloisons dressées de la galerie aux feux.

SOIR HISTORIQUE

En quelque soir, par exemple, que se trouve le touriste naïf, retiré de nos horreurs économiques, la main d'un maître anime le clavecin des prés; on joue aux cartes au fond de l'étang, miroir évocateur des reines et des mignonnes; on a les saintes, les voiles, et les fils d'harmonie, et les chromatismes légendaires, sur le couchant.

Il frissonne au passage des chasses et des hordes. La comédie goutte sur les tréteaux de gazon. Et l'embarras des pauvres et des faibles sur ces plans stupides!

À sa vision esclave, l'Allemagne s'échafaude vers des lunes; les déserts tartares s'éclairent; les révoltes anciennes grouillent dans le centre du Céleste Empire; par les escaliers et les fauteuils de rois—un petit monde blême et plat, Afrique et Occidents, va s'édifier. Puis un ballet de mers et de nuits connues, une chimie sans valeur, et des mélodies impossibles.

La même magie bourgeoise à tous les points où la malle nous déposera! Le plus élémentaire physicien sent qu'il n'est plus possible de se soumettre à cette atmosphère personnelle, brume de remords physiques, dont la constatation est déjà une affliction.

Non! Le moment de l'étuve, des mers enlevées, des embrasements souterrains, de la planète emportée, et des exterminations conséquentes, certitudes si peu malignement indiquées dans la Bible et par les Nornes et qu'il sera donné à l'être sérieux de surveiller.—Cependant ce ne sera point un effet de légende!

BOTTOM

La réalité étant trop épineuse pour mon grand caractère,—je me trouvai néanmoins chez Madame, en gros oiseau gris bleu s'essorant vers les moulures du plafond et traînant l'aile dans les ombres de la soirée.

Je fus, au pied du baldaquin supportant ses bijoux adorés et ses chefs-d'œuvre physiques, un gros ours aux gencives violettes et au poil chenu de chagrin, les yeux aux cristaux et aux argents des consoles.

Tout se fit ombre et aquarium ardent. Au matin,—aube de juin batailleuse,— je courus aux champs, âne, claironnant et brandissant mon grief, jusqu'à ce que les Sabines de la banlieue vinrent se jeter à mon poitrail.

H

Toutes les monstruosités violent les gestes atroces d'Hortense. Sa solitude est la mécanique érotique, sa lassitude, la dynamique amoureuse. Sous la surveillance d'une enfance, elle a été, à des époques nombreuses, l'ardente hygiène des races. Sa porte est ouverte à la misère. Là, la moralité des êtres actuels se décorpore en sa passion, ou en son action.— Ô terrible frisson des amours novices sur le sol sanglant et par l'hydrogène clarteux! trouvez Hortense.

MOUVEMENT

Le mouvement de lacet sur la berge des chutes du fleuve,
Le gouffre à l'étambot,
La célérité de la rampe,
L'énorme passade du courant
Mènent par les lumières inouïes
Et la nouveauté chimique
Les voyageurs entourés des trombes du val
Et du strom.

Ce sont les conquérants du monde
Cherchant la fortune chimique personnelle;
Le sport et le comfort voyagent avec eux;
Ils emmènent l'éducation
Des races, des classes et des bêtes, sur ce Vaisseau.
Repos et vertige
À la lumière diluvienne,
Aux terribles soirs d'étude.

Car de la causerie parmi les appareils,—le sang, les fleurs, le feu, les
    bijoux,—
Des comptes agités à ce bord fuyard,
On voit, roulant comme une digue au delà de la route hydraulique motrice:
Monstrueux, s'éclairant sans fin,—leur stock d'études;
Eux chassés dans l'extase harmonique,
Et l'héroïsme de la découverte.
Aux accidents atmosphériques les plus surprenants
Un couple de jeunesse s'isole sur l'arche,
—Est-ce ancienne sauvagerie qu'on pardonne?
Et chante et se poste.

GÉNIE

Il est l'affection et le présent puisqu'il a fait la maison ouverte à l'hiver écumeux et à la rumeur de l'été, lui qui a purifié les boissons et les aliments, lui qui est le charme des lieux fuyants et le délice surhumain des stations. Il est l'affection et l'avenir, la force et l'amour que nous, debout dans les rages et les ennuis, nous voyons passer dans le ciel de tempête et les drapeaux d'extase.

Il est l'amour, mesure parfaite et réinventée, raison merveilleuse et imprévue, et l'éternité: machine aimée des qualités fatales. Nous avons tous eu l'épouvante de sa concession et de la nôtre: ô jouissance de notre santé, élan de nos facultés, affection égoïste et passion pour lui, lui qui nous aime pour sa vie infinie…

Et nous nous le rappelons et il voyage…Et si l'Adoration s'en va, sonne, sa promesse sonne: «Arrière ces superstitions, ces anciens corps, ces ménages et ces âges. C'est cette époque-ci qui a sombré!»

Il ne s'en ira pas, il ne redescendra pas d'un ciel, il n'accomplira pas la rédemption des colères de femmes et des gaîtés des hommes et de tout ce péché: car c'est fait, lui étant, et étant aimé.

Ô ses souffles, ses têtes, ses courses; la terrible célérité de la perfection des formes et de l'action.

Ô fécondité de l'esprit et immensité de l'univers!

Son corps! le dégagement rêvé, le brisement de la grâce croisée de violence nouvelle!

Sa vue, sa vue! tous les agenouillages anciens et les peines *relevés* à sa suite.

Son jour! l'abolition de toutes souffrances sonores et mouvantes dans la musique plus intense.

Son pas! les migrations plus énormes que les anciennes invasions.

Ô Lui et nous! l'orgueil plus bienveillant que les charités perdues.

Ô monde! et le chant clair des malheurs nouveaux!

Il nous a connus tous et nous a tous aimés. Sachons, cette nuit d'hiver, de cap en cap, du pôle tumultueux au château, de la foule à la plage, de regards en regards, forces et sentiments las, le héler et le voir, et le renvoyer, et, sous les marées et au haut des déserts de neige, suivre ses vues, ses souffles, son corps, son jour.

Self-portrait, Rimbaud, c. 1883.

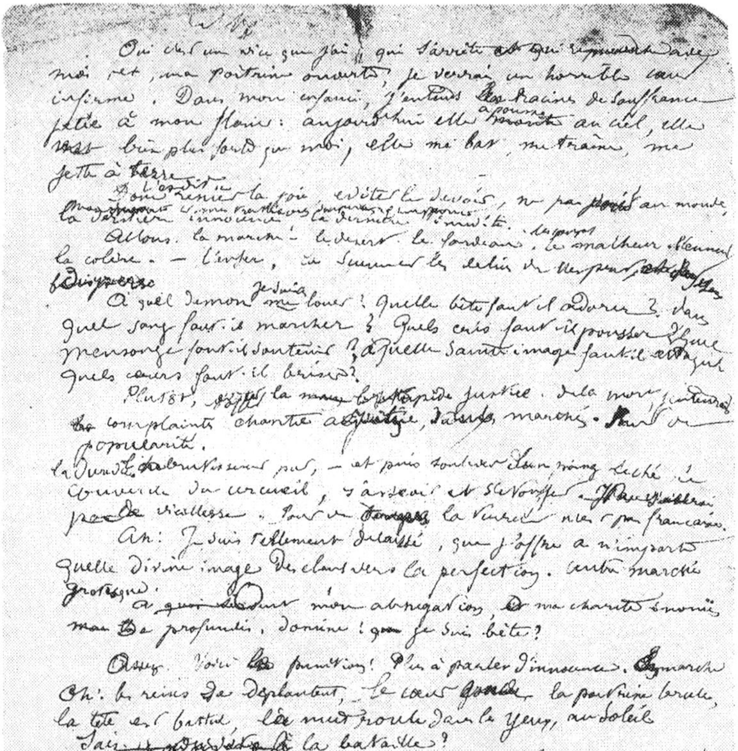

An early draft of Une saison en enfer.

BROUILLON D'*UNE SAISON EN ENFER*

✒

MAUVAIS SANG

Oui c'est un vice que j'ai, qui s'arrête et qui ~~reprend~~ avec moi, et, ma poitrine ouverte, je verrais un horrible cœur infirme. Dans mon enfance, j'entends ses racines de souffrance jetée à mon flanc: aujourd'hui elle a ~~poussé~~ au ciel, elle bien plus forte que moi, elle me bat, me traîne, me jette à terre.

Donc c'est dit, renier la joie, éviter le devoir, ne pas porter au monde mon dégoût et mes trahisons supérieures la dernière innocence, la dernière timidité.

Allons, la marche! le désert, le fardeau, les coups, le malheur, l'ennui, la colère.—L'enfer, là sûrement les délires de mes peurs et se disperse.

À quel démon ~~je suis à~~ me louer? Quelle bête faut-il adorer? dans quel sang faut-il marcher? Quels cris faut-il pousser? Quel mensonge faut-il soutenir? ~~A~~ Quelle Sainte image faut-il attaquer? Quels cœurs faut-il briser?

Plutôt ~~éviter d'offrir la main br~~ stupide justice, de la mort. J'entendrai ~~les la~~ complainte chantée ~~aujourd'hui~~ jadis ~~dans~~ sur les marchés. Point de popularité.

La dure vie, l'abrutissement pur,—et puis soulever d'un poing séché le couvercle du cercueil, s'asseoir et s'étouffer. ~~Je ne vieillirai~~ pas de vieillesse. Point de dangers la terreur n'est pas française.

Ah! je suis tellement délaissé, que j'offre à n'importe quelle divine image des élans vers la perfection. Autre marché grotesque.

~~À quoi servent~~ Ô mon abnégation Ô ma charité inouïes De profundis Domine! je suis bête?

Assez. Voici la punition! Plus à parler d'innocence. En marche. Oh! les reins se déplantent, le cœur gronde, la poitrine brûle, la tête est battue, la nuit roule dans les yeux, au Soleil.

~~Sais-je où je vais~~ Où va-t-on, à la bataille?

Ah! mon âme ma sale jeunesse. Va!... va, les autres avancent ~~remuent~~ les outils, les armes.

Oh! oh. C'est la faiblesse, c'est la bêtise, moi!

Allons, feu sur moi. Ou je me rends! ~~qu'on laisse~~ blessé, je me jette à plat ventre, foulé aux pieds des chevaux.

Ah!

Je m'y habituerai.

Ah çà, je mènerais la vie française, et je tiendrais le Sentier de l'honneur.

FAUSSE CONVERSION

Jour de malheur! J'ai avalé un fameux ~~verre~~ gorgée de poison. La rage du désespoir m'emporte contre tout la nature les objets, moi, que je veux déchirer. Trois fois béni soit le conseil qui m'est arrivé. ~~M~~ Les entrailles me brûlent, la violence du venin tord mes membres, me rend difforme. Je meurs de soif. J'étouffe. Je ne puis crier. C'est l'enfer l'éternité de la peine. Voilà comme le feu se relève. Va, démon, va, diable, va Satan attise-le. Je brûle ~~bien~~ comme il faut, c'est un bon (bel et bon) enfer.

J'avais entrevu ~~le salut~~ la conversion, le bien, le bonheur, le salut. Puis-je décrire la vision, on n'est pas poète ~~dans~~ en enfer.

~~Dès que~~ C'était ~~l'apparition~~ des milliers de ~~'Apsaras?~~ charmantes, un admirable concert spirituel, la force et la paix, les nobles ambitions, que sais-je!

Ah: les nobles ambitions! ma haine. ~~R~~ Je recommence l'existence enragée la colère dans le sang, la vie bestiale, l'abêtissement, le ~~malheur... mon malh et les malheurs des autres~~ qui m'importe peu et c'est encore la vie! Si la damnation est éternelle. C'est ~~encore la vie encore~~. C'est l'exécution des lois religieuses pourquoi a-t-on semé une foi pareille dans mon esprit? ~~On a Les~~ Mes parents ont fait mon malheur, et le leur, ce qui m'importe peu. On a abusé de mon innocence. Oh! l'idée du baptême. Il y en a qui ont vécu mal, qui vivent mal, et qui ne sentent rien! C'est ~~le~~ mon baptême et ma faiblesse dont je suis esclave. C'est la vie encore!

Plus tard, les délices de la damnation seront plus profondes. Je reconnais bien la damnation. ~~Quand~~ Un homme qui veut se mutiler est bien damné, n'est-ce pas? Je me crois en enfer, donc j'y suis.—Un crime, vite, que je tombe au néant, par la loi des hommes.

Tais-toi. Mais tais-toi! C'est la honte et le reproche, ~~qui~~ à côté de moi; c'est Satan qui me dit que son feu est ignoble, idiot; et que ma colère est affreusement laide. Assez. Tais-toi! ce sont des erreurs qu'on me souffle à l'oreille, ~~la~~ les magies, ~~l'~~ les alchimies, les mysticismes, les parfums ~~fleuris?~~ faux, les musiques naïves, ~~les~~. C'est Satan qui se charge de cela. Alors les poètes sont damnés. Non ce n'est pas cela.

Et dire que je tiens la vérité. Que j'ai un jugement sain et arrêté sur toute chose, que je suis tout prêt pour la perfection. ~~Tais toi, c'est~~ l'orgueil! à présent. Je ne suis qu'un bonhomme en bois, la peau de ma tête se dessèche. Ô Dieu! mon Dieu! mon Dieu! J'ai peur, pitié. Ah! j'ai soif. Ô mon enfance, mon village, les prés, le lac sur la grève le clair de lune quand le clocher sonnait douze. ~~Satan a ri~~. Et c'est au clocher.—Que je deviens bête! Ô Marie, Sainte-Vierge, faux sentiment, fausse prière.

DÉLIRES II: ALCHIMIE DU VERBE

Enfin mon esprit devin[t]. . . . . . .
de Londres ou de Pékin, ou Ber. . . . . . .
qui ~~disparaissent je plaisante sur~~. . . . . . .
de réjouissance populaire. ~~Voilà~~. . . . . . .
les ~~petits~~ fournaises. . . . . . .
J'aurais voulu le désert crayeux de. . . .

J'adorai les boissons tiédies, les boutiques fanées, les vergers brûlés. Je restais de longues heures la langue pendante, comme les bêtes harassées: je me traînais dans les ruelles puantes, et, les yeux fermés, je ~~priais le~~ m'offrais au soleil, Dieu de feu, qu'il me renversât ~~et~~, Général, roi, disais-je, si tu as encore un vieux canons sur tes remparts qui dégringolent, bombarde les hommes avec des ~~monceau~~ mottes de terre sèche Aux glaces des magasins splendides! Dans les salons frais! Que les ~~araignées~~ À ~~la~~ manger sa poussière à la ville! Oxyde des gargouilles. À l'heure exacte après boudoirs ~~du~~ brules sable de rubis les

~~Je portais des vêtements de toile.~~ Je me ~~mot illisible~~ j'allais cassais ~~sie~~ des pierres sur des routes balayées toujours. Le soleil souverain ~~descendait~~ donnait vers ~~la~~ une merde, dans la vallée de la ~~illisible~~, son moucheron enivré au centre
à la pissotière de l'auberge isolée, amoureux de la bourrache,

      et dissous   au soleil
et
      qui va se fondre en un rayon

FAIM

J'ai réfléchis aux bonheur des bêtes; les chenilles étaient les foule ~~pe-tits corps blancs~~ innocen des limbes: romantique envahie par l'aube opale; la punaise, brune personne, attendait ~~mots illisibles~~ passionné. Heureuse ~~le somm~~ la taupe, sommeil de toute la Virginité!

Je m'éloignais ~~du contact~~ Étonnante virginité d'essay l'écrire, avec une espèce de romance. Chanson de la plus haute tour.

Je crus avoir trouvé raison et bonheur. J'écartais le ciel, l'azur, qui est du noir, et je vivais, étincelle d'or de la lumière *nature*. C'était très sérieux. J'exprimai, ~~le plus~~ bêtement.

ÉTERNITÉ

~~Et pour comble~~ De joie, je devins un opéra fabuleux.

ÂGE D'OR

À cette ~~période, c'était~~ c'était ma vie éternelle, non écrite, non chantée,—quelque chose comme la Providence ~~les lois du monde un~~ à laquelle on croit et qui ne chante pas.

Après ces nobles minutes, ~~vint~~ stupidité complète. Je ~~m~~ vis une fatalité de bonheur dans tous les êtres: l'action n'était ~~pas la vie mauvaise~~ qu'une façon ~~de~~ instinctive de gâcher une insatiété de vie: ~~seulement moi, je laissai la sachant~~, au hasard sinistre et doux, ~~un~~ énervement, ~~déviation~~ errement. Le savoir était la faiblesse et la cervelle. . . . .
. . . . êtres et toutes choses m'apparaissaient
. . . . d'autres vies autour d'elles. Ce monsieur
. . . . un ange. Cette famille n'est pas
. . . . Avec plusieurs hommes
. . . . moment d'une de leurs autres vies.
. . . . . . ~~histoire~~ plus de principes. Pas un des sophismes qui. . . . . . . .la folie enfermée.

Je pourrais les redire tous ~~et d'autres~~ et bien d'autres ~~et d'autres~~, je sais le système. Je n'éprouvais plus rien. Les ~~hallucinations étaient tourbillonnaient trop~~. Mais maintenant je ~~ne voudrais~~ n'essaierais pas de me faire écouter.

Un mois de cet exercice, ~~je crus~~ Ma santé ~~s'ébranla~~ fut menacée.

J'avais bien autre chose à faire que de vivre. Les hallucinations étaient plus vives ~~plus épouvantes~~ la terreur ~~plus~~ venait! Je faisais des sommeils de plusieurs jours, et, levé, continuais les rêves les plus tristes (les égarés) partout.

MÉMOIRE

Je me trouvais mûr pour ~~la mort~~ le trépas et ma faiblesse me tirait jusqu'aux confins du monde et de la vie, ~~où le tourbillon~~ dans la Cimmérie noire, patrie des morts, où un grand … a pris une route de dangers laissé presque toute chez une sur emb … tion épouvantes.

CONFINS DU MONDE

Je voyageai un peu. J'allai au nord: je ~~rappelai au~~ (fermai mon cerveau) Je voulus reconnaître là toutes mes odeurs féodales, bergères, sources sauvages. J'aimais la mer ~~bonhomme le sol et les principes~~ l'anneau magique dans l'eau lumineuse ~~éclairée~~ comme si elle dût me laver d'un ~~me laver de ces aberrations~~ souillures. Je voyais la croix consolante. J'avais été damné par l'arc-en-ciel et les ~~bes~~ magies religieuses; et par le Bonheur, ~~mon remor~~ ma fatalité, mon ver, et qui ~~je~~ quoique ~~le monde me parut très nouveau, à moi qui avais~~ levé toutes les impressions possibles: faisant ma vie trop immense énervait même après que ma ~~illisible~~ pour armer (sincer) (seulement) bien réellement la force et la beauté.

Dans les plus grandes villes, à l'aube, ad ~~diluculum~~ matutinum, au Christus venit, ~~quand pour les hommes forts le Christ vient~~ sa dent, douce à ~~la~~ mort, m'avertissait avec le chant du coq.

BONR

Si faible, je ne me crus plus supportable dans la société, qu'à force de
~~pitié~~ Quel malheur Quel cloître possible pour ce beau dégoût?
Cela s'est passé peu à peu.
Je hais maintenant les élans mystiques et les bizarreries de style.
Maintenant je puis dire que l'art est une sottise.
Nos grands poètes aussi facile: l'art est une sottise.
Salut à la bont.

From Rimbaud's school notebook, age eleven.

ACKNOWLEDGMENTS

The images used in this edition are reproduced from the facsimile edition of Rimbaud's work by Steve Murphy (*Œuvres complètes, IV: Fac-similes,* Honoré Champion) and from the definitive biography of the poet by Jean-Jacques Lefrère (*Arthur Rimbaud,* Fayard). I am grateful to these scholar-authors for their generosity with permissions and their patience in unpacking many particulars of Rimbaud's life and work.

Thank you to Roger Stuart Berkowitz and John Jeremiah Sullivan for responding to early drafts of the introduction; and to David Bezmozgis and Charles Bock for offering timely, clarifying edits. All four are demanding readers and exemplary writers. I am grateful for their attention and friendship.

At the Modern Library, I am lucky once again to benefit from the vision and exactitude of Vincent La Scala; the energy and support of Will Murphy; the example of David Ebershoff; and the encouragement of Daniel Menaker.

For their support, in various forms, to the activity of translation and the activities of this translator: Esther Allen, Michael Attias, Peter Gay, Richard Howard, Wendy Lesser, Rick Moody, Roger Shattuck, Anna Stein, Lorin Stein, and Jean Strouse—to all, thank you.

To Suzanne and William Mason, my love.

—WM
Spring 2005

A NOTE ON SOURCES

In the Introduction, quotations sprinkled throughout in Rimbaud's voice are drawn from my translations of his letters (*Rimbaud Complete, Volume II: I Promise to Be Good*).

Additional sources, below, are provided for those readers who might wish to learn more about various factual details mentioned in passing.

p. xvii   Salacious tidbits about Rimbaud's life (arrests, vagrancy, stabbing) are a feature of all biographies of the poet. In English, accounts by Starkie, Robb, and Steinmetz all contain versions of these factual details. In French, their accounting by Jean-Jacques Lefrère is more dependably even-tempered (and a better read).

Rimbaud's visit to the Round Reading Room is known to us because of the existence of the document that appears on this page. Otherwise, information relating to Rimbaud and Verlaine's time in London is largely hearsay. Documents (including advertisements placed in newspapers; business cards they had printed; envelopes they addressed) all attest to their locations and hint at their activities during their London stays. Letters and journals by various of their friends and family in England and France add to our picture of their time there but cannot be considered dependable, only suggestive. A little bit more about this period may be read in Robb (pp. 183–206) and Lefrère (pp. 521–561).

A useful article by Angeline Goureau about the history of the Round Reading Room can be read online in *The New York Times* (November 9, 1997): http://www.nytimes.com/books/97/11/09/bookend/bookend.html?

p. xviii   Lenin's lie is known to us via a letter dated 21 April 1902 that he wrote to the Library Director. An excellent account of the machinations surrounding his pseudonym may be read online at the website of the British Library: http://www.bl.uk/collections/easteuropean/lenin.html

Rimbaud's supposed pornographic misbehaviors (writing on café tables with his excrement; ejaculating on inappropriate objects) come from highly undependable anecdotes that pepper letters and diaries of various literary figures of the day. Too often, they are passed off as fact in contemporary biographies of the poet (when not distorted altogether). A fuller discussion of this unfortunate tendency to mythologize Rimbaud may be found in my "The Elaborations: Rimbaud at the Mercy of His Biographers" (*Harper's,* October 2002).

p. xix The exact nature of the illness that led to Rimbaud's death is a subject that keeps biographers busy. Like the exact state of Van Gogh's mental health, everyone has a theory.

p. xxii Ezra Pound's poetical ideas and ideals are dispersed through many of his works. Readers could profitably consult both *An ABC of Reading* and *Confucius to Cummings.* Also, there is always *The Cantos,* Pound's own poem with history.

p. xxiv More of Baudelaire's essay may be read in *The Painter of Modern Life and Other Essays,* well translated and edited by Jonathan Mayne. The quote used here can be found on page 12.

SELECTED BIBLIOGRAPHY

FRENCH EDITIONS OF RIMBAUD'S WORKS
Œuvres complètes. De Renéville and Mouquet, eds. Gallimard, Pléiade, 1954.
Œuvres complètes. Antoine Adam, ed. Gallimard, Pléiade, 1972.
Œuvre/vie. Alain Borer, ed. Arléa, 1991.
Œuvres complètes. Pierre Brunel, ed. Livre de Poche, 1999.
Œuvres complètes, I: Poésies. Steve Murphy, ed. Honoré Champion, 1999.
Œuvres complètes, IV: Fac-similies. Steve Murphy, ed. Honoré Champion, 2002.

ENGLISH TRANSLATIONS OF RIMBAUD'S WORKS
Collected Poems. Oliver Bernard, tr. Penguin, 1962.
Complete Works, Selected Letters. Wallace Fowlie, tr. Chicago, 1966.
Complete Works. Paul Schmidt, tr. Harper & Row, 1976.
Rimbaud: The Works. Dennis J. Carlile, tr. Xlibris, 2000.
Collected Poems. Martin Sorrell, tr. Oxford University Press, 2001.
Rimbaud Complete. Wyatt Mason, tr. Modern Library, 2002.

ON RIMBAUD'S POETRY AND LIFE
A Concordance to the Œuvres complètes of Arthur Rimbaud. William Carter and Robert Vines, eds. Ohio University Press, 1978.
Berrichon, Paterne. *Arthur Rimbaud, Poète.* Mercure de France, 1912.
Cohn, Robert Greer. *The Poetry of Rimbaud.* University of South Carolina Press, 1999.
Delahaye, Ernest. *Delahaye témoin de Rimbaud.* Baconnière, 1974.
Izambard, Georges. *Rimbaud tel que je l'ai connu.* Le passeur, 1991.
Jeancolas, Claude. *Les lettres manuscrites de Rimbaud.* Textuel, 1997.
Lefrère, Jean-Jacques. *Arthur Rimbaud.* Fayard, 2001.

Lefrère, Jean-Jacques, et al. *Rimbaud à Aden.* Fayard, 2001.

———. *Rimbaud à Harar.* Fayard, 2002.

Robb, Graham. *Rimbaud.* Norton, 2000.

Starkie, Enid. *Rimbaud.* Norton, 1947.

Steinmetz, Jean-Luc. *Une Question de presence.* Tallandier, 1999.

ON SUBJECTS RELATING TO TRANSLATION

Baudelaire, Charles. *Les Fleurs du Mal.* Richard Howard, tr. Godine, 1980.

———. *The Painter of Modern Life.* Jonathan Mayne, tr. Da Capo Press, 1964.

Borges, Jorge Luis. *This Craft of Verse.* Harvard, 2000.

Craft and Context of Translation. William Arrowsmith and Roger Shattuck, eds. University of Texas Press, 1961.

Davenport, Guy. *Seven Greeks.* New Directions, 1995.

Gass, William. *Reading Rilke.* Ecco, 2000.

Random House Book of Twentieth-Century French Poetry. Paul Auster, ed. Random House, 1981.

Rilke, Rainer Maria. *Selected Poetry.* Stephen Mitchell, tr. Vintage, 1983.

ABOUT THE TRANSLATOR

WYATT MASON is a contributing editor of *Harper's* magazine, where his essays regularly appear. He also writes for *The London Review of Books* and *The New Republic*. The Modern Library has published his translations of the complete works of Arthur Rimbaud in two volumes. His translations of Dante's *Vita Nuova* and Montaigne's *Essais* are in progress.

A NOTE ON THE TYPE

The principal text of this Modern Library edition
was set in a digitized version of Janson, a typeface that
dates from about 1690 and was cut by Nicholas Kis,
a Hungarian working in Amsterdam. The original matrices have
survived and are held by the Stempel foundry in Germany.
Hermann Zapf redesigned some of the weights and sizes for
Stempel, basing his revisions on the original design.

Modern Library is online at
WWW.MODERNLIBRARY.COM

MODERN LIBRARY ONLINE IS YOUR GUIDE
TO CLASSIC LITERATURE ON THE WEB

THE MODERN LIBRARY E-NEWSLETTER

Our free e-mail newsletter is sent to subscribers, and features sample chapters, interviews with and essays by our authors, upcoming books, special promotions, announcements, and news. To subscribe to the Modern Library e-newsletter, visit **www.modernlibrary.com**

THE MODERN LIBRARY WEBSITE

Check out the Modern Library website at
www.modernlibrary.com for:

- The Modern Library e-newsletter
- A list of our current and upcoming titles and series
- Reading Group Guides and exclusive author spotlights
- Special features with information on the classics and other paperback series
- Excerpts from new releases and other titles
- A list of our e-books and information on where to buy them
- The Modern Library Editorial Board's 100 Best Novels and 100 Best Nonfiction Books of the Twentieth Century written in the English language
- News and announcements

Questions? E-mail us at **modernlibrary@randomhouse.com**.
For questions about examination or desk copies, please visit
the Random House Academic Resources site at
www.randomhouse.com/academic

THE BEST OF THE MODERN LIBRARY IN TRANSLATION

Alexandre Dumas
The Knight of Maison-Rouge
Translated by Julie Rose, with an
Introduction by Lorenzo Carcaterra
Trade Paperback: 978-0-8129-6963-4

"Dumas seduces, fascinates, entertains,
and instructs. His works are so diverse,
so varied, so alive, so charming, so
powerful; they radiate that light that
is so peculiar to France."
—Victor Hugo

Emile Zola
The Kill
(Finalist for the French-American
Foundation Translation Prize)

Translated, with an Introduction,
by Arthur Goldhammer
Trade Paperback: 978-0-8129-6637-4

"Goldhammer's translation of Zola's
satiric, transgressive tale—about,
among other things, Paris, modernity
incest, and the order of the new—is a
work of pure delight. And his introduc
tion to the novel is simply brilliant." -
—Jean Strouse

Arthur Rimbaud
Rimbaud Complete, Volumes I & II
Translated, edited, and with
Introductions by Wyatt Mason

Vol. I: Poetry and Prose
Trade Paperback: 978-0-375-75770-9

Vol. II: I Promise to Be Good, the Letters of Arthur Rimbaud
Trade Paperback: 978-0-8129-7015-9

"It's quite likely that [the season's] most
exciting new book of verse was stamped
Made in France more than a century
ago.... *Rimbaud Complete*, Wyatt
Mason's bouncy new translation of the
avant-garde poet's hallucinatory corpus,
finds new music in the writing, reveal-
ing a classical artist."
—*Entertainment Weekly*, Editor's Choice, A-

THE BEST OF THE MODERN LIBRARY IN TRANSLATION

Voltaire
Candide

Translated by Peter Constantine, with an Introduction by Diane Johnson

Trade Paperback: 978-0-8129-7201-6

"The major plot elements of *Candide* seem ripped from today's headlines.... Voltaire's work remains almost disturbingly relevant. In her preface to Constantine's translation, Diane Johnson points out the parallels between the religious executions in Voltaire's time and the taped beheadings in Iraq."
—Bloomberg.com

Honoré de Balzac
The Wrong Side of Paris

Translated by Jordan Stump, with an Introduction by Adam Gopnik

Trade Paperback: 978-0-8129-6675-6

"An excellent translation [of] a melodrama akin to *The Count of Monte Cristo* . . . a solid and phantasmagoric picture of Paris."
—A. S. Byatt

Stendhal
The Red and the Black

Translated by Burton Raffel, with an Introduction by Diane Johnson

Trade Paperback: 978-0-8129-7207-8

"[Raffel's] exciting new translation of *The Red and the Black* blasts Stendhal into the 21st century."
—Salon.com

The Charterhouse of Parma
(National Bestseller)

Translated by Richard Howard

Trade Paperback: 978-0-679-78318-3

"[A] superb new translation."
—Bernard Knox, *The New York Review of Books*

Printed in the United States
by Baker & Taylor Publisher Services